She went hot and cold all over. It was as if he'd shone a light into some secret part of her heart and something dark and ugly had crawled out. She *had* rejected Jeff because she didn't want a sick boyfriend. She'd said as much to Katie at Jenny House.

"It's any sickness, Jeff. It's mine too. I hate it all. I know it's not your fault, but it's not mine either."

"I'll bet no one at your school knows you're a diabetic."

She said nothing.

"I'm right, aren't I?"

"It's none of your business."

"You know, Lacey, you're the person who won't accept that you have a disease. Why is that?"

She whirled on him. "How can you ask me that when you've just admitted that girls drop you once they discover you're a bleeder? You of all people should understand why I keep my little secret."

ONE LAST WISH

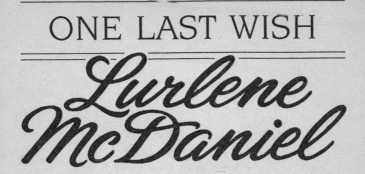

Lurlene McDaniel

All the Days of Her Life

BANTAM BOOKS

NEW YORK · TORONTO · LONDON · SYDNEY · AUCKLAND

RL 5, age 10 and up

ALL THE DAYS OF HER LIFE

A Bantam Book / September 1994

The Starfire logo is a registered trademark of Bantam Books,
a division of Bantam Doubleday Dell Publishing Group, Inc.
Registered in U.S. Patent and Trademark Office and elsewhere.

ISBN 0-553-56264-9

Published simultaneously in the United States and Canada

Bantam Books are published by Bantam Books, a division of Bantam
Doubleday Dell Publishing Group, Inc. Its trademark, consisting of the
words "Bantam Books" and the portrayal of a rooster, is Registered in
U.S. Patent and Trademark Office and in other countries. Marca Regis-
trada. Bantam Books, 1540 Broadway, New York, New York 10036.

PRINTED IN THE UNITED STATES OF AMERICA

RAD   0 9 8 7 6 5 4 3 2 1

For my son, Sean. Twice a day, every day, for all the days of your life.

I would like to thank Gary Klieman and all of the staff of the Diabetes Research Institute, 1450 N.W. 10th Avenue, Miami, Florida 33136, for their invaluable help in the researching of this book. Much is being done to cure diabetes, and the DRI is one of the foremost institutions working in the area of islet cell transplantation today.

One

⌒❤⌒

Lacey Duval sat on her bed hating the filled insulin syringe she held in her hand. Another morning and she needed her shot. The needle made her feel like a prisoner, even though her doctor always said it made her life easier. She'd been a diabetic since she'd turned eleven, so she'd spent five years giving herself twice-a-day shots and of living in fear of untimely insulin reactions. She hated the whole business.

"Lacey!" her mother called from the kitchen. "The phone's for you. It's your friend from Michigan. Don't be too long, or you'll be late for school. I'm leaving for work now. I'll see you after six."

Lacey grabbed the extension on her desk. "Hi," said her friend Katie O'Roark in Ann Arbor. "I know it's early to call, but I wanted you to know we're bringing Chelsea home from the hospital today."

"That's great. How's she doing?"

"So far no problems with organ rejection. Her new heart's working fine."

Lacey was relieved. She'd spent weeks worrying about Chelsea, afraid that her friend's heart transplant would reject and she would die. She shuddered over thoughts about sickness and death. "How's she dealing with Jillian's death?"

"That part's been rougher," Katie confessed. "She was in the pits for weeks and almost lost her will to live. You know that Jillian left Chelsea a videotape and Chelsea played it over and over. I think that helped change her attitude. I think she's crazy about Jillian's brother DJ too. But it looks pretty hopeless for them to get together."

Lacey had met Jillian only once, but the girl had had an impact on her. Lacey felt it wasn't fair that people got sick, or needed organs and there weren't enough to go around to make everyone well. Especially kids. She set down her insulin syringe, loathing it more than ever because it reminded her that although she felt fine, and looked "normal," she was saddled with a disease.

"How long will Chelsea and her mom stay with you before she can go back home?" Lacey asked.

"Another six weeks." Katie paused. "My parents have been great. We'll all miss her when she leaves. She's been living with us since September, so I've gotten used to having her around."

Lacey's bedside clock radio warned her that she

was going to be late for first period, but she didn't cut off the conversation. "How's track coming?"

"The season opens in April. I'll be ready. Right now there's snow on the ground."

"I've read about snow. White stuff that's cold. Here in Miami, it's going to be seventy-five today. I may have to dab on some suntan lotion."

"You're mean!" Katie said with a laugh. "We probably won't see the ground until March."

"How's your little problem with Josh and Garrison working out? It must be hard to have two guys longing for you, although I wouldn't know."

Katie sighed and Lacey sensed her frustration. "Josh still sees red if Garrison so much as talks to me in the hall."

"That's not who I'm asking about. How does Katie feel about Garrison?"

"I wish I'd never mentioned him to you. You ask too many loaded questions."

"Remember what I told you over Thanksgiving break at Jenny House," Lacey answered. "Some guys like to mess with a girl's head. It makes them feel important."

Katie sidestepped Lacey's question. "How about you and Jeff? Did you hear from him over Christmas?"

"Jeff sent me a card from Colorado, but I ignored it."

"You are so cruel, Lacey."

"Don't preach. I know what I'm doing." Like the others in her circle of Jenny House friends, Jeff was also sick, a hemophiliac. Lacey knew she couldn't handle having a sick boyfriend no matter how much she liked him. The clock stared accusingly at her. She was going to be very late. "Listen, much as I hate to cut this short, I've got to go to school."

"I'm sorry to make you late. I miss talking to you."

"Same here. I'll call you and Chelsea on Saturday, when the rates are lower. Tell her I'm really glad she's doing so well."

"Will do."

Lacey hung up, grabbed her books, and headed to the door. She was turning her car into the school parking lot, when she remembered her insulin syringe lying beside the phone. If she returned home for it, she'd be worse than tardy, she'd be given a detention. *All right, so you forgot,* she told herself philosophically. *No big deal.* It wouldn't be the first time. She'd simply cut back on her eating all day and locate near a water fountain to deal with the thirst she knew would come.

By noon her burning thirst seemed unquenchable. Lacey pleaded sickness—in fact, she felt sick to her stomach from high blood sugar—and got out of phys ed. When the school nurse saw her, she sent her home. When Terri Gutierrez saw her in the hall on her way out, Lacey told her, "Touch of the flu." She didn't like fibbing, but there was no way Lacey wanted anyone from school to know she was a diabetic. She'd hidden that tidbit of information and would continue to do so.

"You've got to be better by tomorrow night," Terri insisted, her large brown eyes full of concern.

"Todd's having a blow-out at his place after the basketball game. You know what fun Todd's parties are."

"I'll be fine," Lacey assured her.

By the time she arrived home, Lacey felt awful. She figured her blood sugar was sky high and that ketones, poisonous wastes from lack of insulin, were building in her bloodstream.

She realized that she should test her blood with her glucose monitoring machine, but that would mean pricking the sensitive tip of her finger to squeeze out a drop of blood onto the testing strip. "Forget it," she told herself, deciding instead to try to rid her body of ketones and excessive sugar by drinking large quantities of water and getting insulin into herself as quickly as possible.

She threw away the syringe filled with her morning dose of long-acting insulin and drew up a syringe of regular—short-acting—insulin. She reminded herself that too much would carry the risk of a reaction. And too little wouldn't solve her problem.

With a wince, Lacey inserted the short needle into the fleshy part of her abdomen. She pushed down the plunger, and as the insulin flowed into her, it burned. She withdrew the needle, pressed the site with an antiseptic-drenched cotton ball, and waited for the burning to cease. Finally, she broke off the needle and threw the debris into the garbage.

Her forgetfulness about her morning shot would mean another shot of regular insulin later that evening. Why couldn't medical science figure out a better way to get insulin into a diabetic's body?

Chelsea had once asked if she could qualify for a pancreas transplant—the organ that produced insulin in the body. She'd asked her doctor, who was also her uncle, about the possibility, and he'd shaken his head. "It's not practical. As long as you continue to do well on standard therapy, we won't rock the boat." Then he'd peered over the tops of his glasses and added, "If you'd come to some of the seminars and support group meetings at the hospital, you'd learn about these things."

"I attended some of the meetings," she'd said defensively.

"You came twice."

"Who wants to hang around with a bunch of sickies? I'm not sick," Lacey insisted.

"Lacey, be reasonable. Diabetes is a manageable disease. And support groups can help work out your feelings."

She'd grabbed her purse and ducked out of his office, saying over her shoulder, "I come in for regular checkups with you. That's enough."

The ringing phone made Lacey start. The second she heard her father's voice her stomach constricted. "How's my girl?" he asked. "Are we still on for this weekend? I've gotten us tickets for *Cats* Saturday afternoon at the convention center."

Ever since her parents had separated over the holidays and her father had taken an apartment, he'd been spending time with her by asking her to do things on the weekends. "Sure, Dad, that'll be fine," she heard herself say mechanically. She really didn't want to go. Pretending that she didn't mind about their divorce took too much effort. And both her dad and her mother kept trying to tell her they were *all* better off now that the marriage was over. She didn't understand how they expected her to be happy, but then, she didn't understand her parents anyway.

"I'll pick you up at eleven. We'll have lunch first." She heard him pause. "I—miss you, Lacey."

"I'll be ready," she told him, unwilling to tell him she missed him too, unwilling to say "I love you, Daddy."

Once she hung up, Lacey felt a lump rise in her throat. Late afternoon sun slanted through the curtains and lent the room an air of melancholia. Why couldn't her parents get along? Why did she have to have diabetes? Why did she have to make friends with girls who up and died? *Why?* The questions swirled in her head like a dog chasing its tail.

She forced herself to think about other things. The world of Todd Larson and his friends was normal. Those kids didn't really know about tough decisions. Normalcy was what she wanted for herself. Suddenly, she felt light-headed and realized that her blood sugar was dropping too rapidly. She went to the refrigerator to get orange juice and stave off the reaction fast descending on her. *Life's not fair!* she thought. *It's just not fair!*

Two

Lacey shouldered her way through the crowd of kids swarming around Todd Larson's pool deck area toward Terri, Sheila, and Monet, three other girls from school. "Glad you made it," Terri said. "Are you feeling better today?"

"Perfect." Lacey flashed a smile to prove it. "I had to park two blocks down the street. What a mob scene."

"Todd throws good parties," Monet said with a bored expression. She was a tall, willowy blonde who did some professional modeling. Monet wasn't Lacey's favorite person. Lacey considered her conceited and snobbish, totally unfriendly.

With a sly whisper, Sheila told Lacey, "Get a soda and I'll pour a little something special in it."

Lacey knew she meant something alcoholic because it was obvious that many in the crowd had been drinking. She was tempted, but for diabetics alcohol wasn't smart. It wreaked havoc with blood sugar levels. All she needed was to have a reaction and make a fool of herself in front of her friends. Especially Monet. "Maybe later," she hedged.

"How about you, Terri?" Sheila asked.

"Too many empty calories," Terri said with a grin. "I'd rather waste them on chocolate."

Lacey admired Terri's way of saying no. "So what's happening?" Lacey asked.

The heated pool was thick with swimmers, the lounge chairs filled with couples. Rock music blared from speakers hung in surrounding palm trees. Colored lanterns and spotlights highlighting flower beds and tropical foliage glowed in the spacious, sloping backyard. A high wooden security fence ringed the yard, affording complete privacy from neighbors.

In one direction, Todd's house rose, a two-story mansion of white stucco and red Spanish tile.

"Same old, same old," Monet said. "No new faces. What a bore."

"Then why'd you come?" Terri asked.

"She hopes Todd will give her a tumble," Sheila said cattily.

Lacey didn't like what she heard. She'd secretly been interested in Todd herself ever since school had started in September. Monet was formidable competition.

Monet arched an eyebrow. "I usually get what I go after."

"Did you get that job modeling clothes for the catalogue that's shooting on Miami Beach next week?" Terri asked.

"Of course. My agent called to confirm yesterday."

Terri said, "I'd love to model, but I love food too much." She patted her hips. "And every bite settles here."

"I eat whatever I want," Monet said.

"But you never seem to gain weight."

"There're ways around gaining."

Lacey listened glumly. Her diabetes caused her to wage an endless war with weight gain. The only time she'd been truly thin was when she'd been first diagnosed. Diabetic ketoacidosis, a condition brought on by a need for insulin, had left her weak, gaunt, and dehydrated. She remembered feeling rotten, but at least she'd been thin.

"Why are the best-looking girls at my party standing with one another instead of mingling?" Todd asked, swooping into the foursome, encircling Monet's and Lacey's waists with broad, muscular arms.

Lacey felt her breath catch at the sight of him. Monet said, "We were drawing straws to see who gets you for the evening."

Todd grinned. "Who won?"

"Don't you mean 'Who lost?' "

Todd nuzzled Monet's neck. "I could make time for all of you."

"Sorry, I don't do crowd scenes," Monet told him, eyeing the others. "And three is definitely a crowd."

He pulled back. "If it's privacy you want, come into the house with me."

Lacey felt Todd's arm leave her waist as he turned his full attention onto Monet. "Maybe I will," Monet said coyly. "But you'd better make it worth my time."

Todd took her hand and started up the sloping lawn toward the back patio and veranda of his home. "Don't mind me," Sheila called after Monet, her voice edged with sarcasm. "I'll find another way home." She whirled toward Terri and Lacey, looking miffed. "Monet never thinks of anybody but herself. Did you see how she hustled Todd off?"

"Big deal," Terri said.

But Lacey thought it was a big deal. In one smooth movement, Monet had staked her claim on Todd and wrapped him up like a package. "There's no accounting for taste," Lacey said to the others.

Sheila studied her. "At least you'll be doing his makeup for the play. That'll put you in his face every night for two weeks."

"It's a dirty job, but somebody has to do it," Lacey said sweetly, knowing Sheila's observation was true. The senior play was in March. Rehearsals had already started and soon, full makeup would be required. In the meantime, Lacey painted sets and did backstage work. "I'll mention your name when I'm 'in his face.'"

Sheila stalked off. Lacey watched her clear a path through the crowds and asked, "Gee, was it something I said?"

Terri smiled. "Poor Sheila. Two strikes against her in less than fifteen minutes."

"Are you feeling sorry for her?"

"Are you kidding? She's the biggest mouth in school. She deserves to be hassled." Terri tapped her chin thoughtfully. "Do *you* like Todd?"

"He's all right. Aren't you interested in him?"

"No way. The only person Todd cares about is Todd. He's too good-looking. He has too much money. He thinks he can have anything he wants. Don't waste your time on him, Lacey."

"Nothing else is happening."

"Boredom's no reason to go after a guy."

Terri's words brought back Katie's from the previous summer at Jenny House when Katie had accused Lacey of leading on Jeff McKensie simply because she didn't have anything better to do. Lacey told Terri, "Todd's cute. I'm interested."

"Poor girl. I'm telling you, Todd's no catch."

"Even for Monet?"

"Especially Monet. They're probably up there fighting right now over who gets to use the mirror first."

Lacey chuckled. "So who makes your pulse race from our school?"

"Dakota."

Lacey searched her memory for a face to put with the name. "Do I know a Dakota?"

"Sure. He's my white rat in psychology lab. He's warm and fuzzy and totally dependent on me. He's a cheap date, and when I'm with him, he has eyes only for me. Little beady red eyes full of adoration. Yes, Dakota loves me truly."

"You're silly." Lacey said with a grin. She looked around at the party crowd again. The music had grown louder, the shrieking and laughter louder still. The pool water had sloshed all over the deck, filling the air with the scent of chlorine. Several lounge chairs were sitting on the bottom of the pool and the colored lights, which earlier had seemed so pretty, made things look garish and distorted. All at once she didn't want to be there. "Would you like to come back to my house, make some popcorn, and watch TV? Friday is Fright Night on channel four."

"I'd like that better than staying here," Terri said. "My car's parked someplace out front."

"You can follow me." Lacey led the way out of the party, wondering why she'd never developed a closer friendship with Terri, who seemed nice and fun to be with. She thought fleetingly about Todd and Monet. Perhaps Terri was right. Maybe Todd was too used to getting whatever he wanted. Ruefully, she told herself that tonight, at least, what he wanted wasn't her.

She found her car, waited until Terri drove up behind her, then led the way out of Todd's neighborhood toward her own home miles away. In the rearview mirror, the lights from the party glowed against the night sky while the house where Todd lived reminded her of an amusement park.

* * *

Lacey awoke Saturday morning feeling sluggish and cranky. She blinked at the clock beside her head-board and saw that it was nine-thirty. Her father was picking her up for lunch and the matinee in ninety minutes. She groaned, cross with herself for sleeping so late. Why hadn't her mother called her? Why hadn't she remembered to set her alarm?

Terri had stayed until after midnight, and they'd had fun watching old horror movies and eating popcorn together. When Terri went home, Lacey continued to stay up watching an all-night movie channel. She'd eaten more than she should have and that's why she'd not awakened shaky from an insulin reaction. However, now it was too late for breakfast, since she'd be eating lunch soon. Worst of all, she'd missed her morning injection time.

The regimentation of her diabetes was almost as bad as the shots. The only time in recent memory she'd stuck to a decent schedule had been over the summer at Jenny House. Which reminded her that she'd told Katie she would call today. Feeling over-whelmed, Lacey covered her head with her pillow and screamed. The sound was muffled, but it did make her feel better.

She rolled out of bed, only to hear the doorbell ringing. "Now what?" Where was her mother any-way? As the bell sounded once more, she recalled her mother telling her something about working overtime in order to prepare a presentation for a new client the ad agency she worked for was woo-ing.

"Terrific!" Lacey muttered under her breath. She

pulled a filmy bathrobe around herself, raked her hand through her tangled blond hair, and ran for the door, shouting, "Hold on! I'm coming!"

She yanked open the door and blinked against the glare of the bright morning sun. "What is it—?" She stopped midsentence.

"I like your outfit." Jeff McKensie said, eyeing her up and down. He reached out and touched her cheek. "So, Lacey, have you got a minute for an old friend? Or do I have to stand on your doorstep while you stare me down?"

Three

UNABLE TO DO much except stare, Lacey obediently stepped aside and let him into the foyer of her house.

"Nice place," Jeff said, peering into the living room. "Why don't you close the door? You're letting the warm air out."

Lacey shut the door, for although the sun was shining brightly, the January day had dawned cool and seemed destined to remain so. Recovering from the shock of seeing Jeff on her doorstep, she asked, "What are you doing in Miami? I thought you were in Colorado."

"I transferred to the University of Miami for winter term. It has a top-notch program for my major —architecture. If you'd written me back instead of ignoring my Christmas card, I'd have told you."

She ignored his barb. "Are you here just for this term?"

"For my final two years of undergraduate work, actually. I've rented an apartment near the campus. I'll show it to you sometime."

"How long have you been in town?"

"Three days. I drove. Hauled all my junk in a trailer across half the United States. But I'm settled in now. Classes start Monday, so since I have a weekend to kill, I thought I'd look you up."

Lacey heard the sound of her heart thudding and wasn't sure if it was thumping in joy over seeing him again, or in fear, because he was part of a world she didn't want to be reminded of. "I didn't know you wanted to be an architect."

"There's lots you don't know about me. Lots I want you to know."

The way his green eyes bore into her made color creep up her neck. She recalled the explosions of heat she'd felt when he'd kissed her in the woods near Jenny House on the Fourth of July, and suddenly realized that she was still in her nightgown and robe. She clutched the top of the robe closer to her throat. "It was nice of you to drop by but you really should have called me first," she said in her frostiest voice. "I'm sure you'll be happy at U of M. I've—uh—got a date, so I can't talk now."

His eyebrow arched. "A date in the middle of the day?"

Flustered, she realized that she'd wanted him to think the date was more than it was, but at the last moment she chickened out. "My dad's taking me to lunch and a play. My parents split up over the holidays."

"I'm sorry."

She shrugged and turned her head away, hoping he hadn't seen the mist that had sprung to her eyes. "No big deal. It's been coming for months. Living here for the past few years was like living in a war zone. Now that Dad's moved out, things are much more peaceful."

"You might have said something about it this summer."

"It wasn't anyone's business." She tossed her long blond hair to make her point. She didn't want his pity, and she didn't want him knowing too much about her. "And Jenny House was far away, so I didn't have to think about it during the summer. Once I got home, school started. I kept busy."

"You wrote me one letter last September," Jeff said. "A kissoff, if I recall. You didn't mention it then either."

"I don't owe you any explanations about my personal life, Jeff. And since you brought up the letter, I *did* intend it to end contact between us."

"No joke," he said without humor. "It would have worked, except I knew I was transferring colleges and since we'll be in the same city—"

"Miami's a huge city. No reason for us to run into each other."

"You're the only person I know here."

He looked lonely and maybe even homesick. She

had an instantaneous picture of herself being delivered to Jenny House against her will and remembered what it felt like to be alone and abandoned far away from everything that was familiar. Except for Katie's determination to make her a part of the group, Lacey would have had the most miserable summer of her life instead of one of her best. She felt contrite over the way she was treating him. He deserved better. "Jeff, I didn't mean to say you're unwelcome. It's just that I have a life."

"Hey—so do I. I'm not out to crowd you. It's just that we were friends at Jenny House. We shared a pretty deep experience with Amanda, and I guess I'm feeling that still connects us someway."

Amanda Burdick had been everybody's friend, and when her leukemia had returned and she'd been hospitalized, Lacey and her friends had visited her faithfully. Lacey found it difficult to think about her. "Mandy loved you," Lacey said, feeling a lump of loss and regret lodge in her throat.

"And I did everything I could to make her think I loved her too. And I *did* love her," Jeff added with conviction.

"But not in the way she thought you did."

"She was like a sister to me. And don't forget, she was just thirteen. I'm almost nineteen. In the best of circumstances, it would have been a bad case of puppy love."

"Except that the puppy died."

"Low blow, Lacey." Jeff's expression looked wounded.

Lacey regretted her stinging words. But then, she'd always had a problem biting her tongue when she was rattled or caught off balance. And Jeff's sudden appearance had definitely caught her off balance. And so had the memories he'd stirred up. "Sorry," she said.

"Can we call a truce?"

Frustration and guilt bombarded her. Last summer, in spite of her vow to have nothing to do with a guy with medical problems, she'd begun to care about Jeff. Then Katie had dropped the news about Amanda's crush on him. Lacey reminded herself that she'd done the right thing—she'd backed away from Jeff and kept a hands-off policy for the duration of Amanda's illness. And once Amanda was gone, she had decided it would be best to forget Jeff completely. He would always be a hemophiliac, and she knew how horribly painful it was to lose somebody you loved. "Truce," she said.

He caught her hand. "Can we seal the treaty with a date? I'd like to think I had a friend in this town."

His touch sent a jolt through her, but she was careful not to react. She understood his feelings of loneliness, of needing company. She felt torn, but said, "I guess so. Just for old time's sake."

"What else?"

"I don't know what I can give you, Jeff. I'm pretty busy with school and all."

"Don't be afraid of me. I won't be a bother."

She was afraid of falling for him again but didn't dare let him know. "You'll be busy with college and I'll be busy with my life. No problem."

Jeff gave her a speculative look. "Then what's the harm of spending a little time together?"

"No harm," she conceded. If she attempted to tell him otherwise, she'd be impossibly late.

"Then I'll call you later." He grinned and reached behind him for the doorknob. "But first—" With a quick movement he pulled her into his arms, kissed her longingly, and slipped out of the house.

It happened too fast for her to push him away. The only sensation she felt as she watched him jog toward his car was surprise. Surprise over how the warmth of his lips lingered on her mouth like sunshine. Surprise over how much she wanted to kiss him again.

"You're not eating much," her father said. He and Lacey were sitting in a nice restaurant, the kind that spread double tablecloths and sported fresh flowers in clear glass vases on every tabletop. She realized that when her parents had been together they'd not gone out to fancy restaurants much.

"I'm trying to lose a few pounds," she said. "Too much pigging out over the holidays."

"You're not fat. You have a nice shape."

"Maybe for Miss Piggy."

Her father's face clouded with concern. "But—um—what about your diabetes? I wouldn't want you to have problems. Is your mother helping you? Or is she avoiding her responsibilities?"

"Mom's doing fine, Dad. I've had diabetes for five years and I know what I'm doing." She couldn't ever remember her father taking an active role in managing her disease. He had been scared when she'd been first diagnosed, hovering over her during her initial hospitalization but turning pasty white when asked to learn how to give her an insulin injection. Her mother had learned, in case of an emergency, but it was Lacey who'd managed her illness from the very beginning.

"I only want to make sure she's supporting you."

She almost told him that neither he nor her mother knew the meaning of the word. "Support" from her mother was nagging Lacey about blood sugar testing and forbidden foods she tried sneaking. And her father's "support" was to hide behind his newspaper when she gave herself shots or complain to his wife because he didn't like the meals she'd prepared or her busy work schedule.

She looked at her father and patiently said, "I've been taking care of my situation for years, haven't I? So I should know what I can do and can't do, shouldn't I?"

He nodded, looking relieved. "I do worry about you, honey. You believe that, don't you?"

"Why worry?" She answered his question with one of her own. It seemed to her that if he was so concerned about her health, he would have been more attentive, less detached. And he'd still be living at home. "I'm sixteen. I can handle my life. Besides, it's only diabetes. It's not like cancer or anything."

He reached over and squeezed her hand. "You've

grown up so fast. Right before my eyes. I hope you'll be all right."

She extricated her hand and picked up her fork. She stabbed a wedge of tomato and offered him a smile that felt stiff and forced. "I'm fine, Daddy. Perfectly fine. Don't worry about me one little bit."

Four

⌒⌒

"WHAT DO YOU think of my place?" Jeff turned on a lamp and ushered Lacey inside his apartment.

She glanced around a room furnished with mismatched pieces of rental furniture and top-of-the-line stereo equipment. In one corner there were stacks of books and rolled-up posters. In another, piles of clothes were heaped on cardboard boxes. A half wall separated the living room area from a tiny kitchen. All walls were painted either coral or turquoise.

"Of course, there's still stuff to do," he explained as he cleared a spot on the sofa for her to sit. "I plan to buy some boards and bricks to make bookshelves along that wall." He pointed.

Lacey circled the room, saw a collection of framed photos, and sorted through them. They consisted of panoramic scenes of snowcapped mountains and gorgeous sun-streaked skies. "These are good."

"Thanks. My hobby is photography."

"I'm impressed."

He grinned. "If I'd known that's all it took, I'd have shown you my work months ago."

She returned to the sofa. The cushions felt squishy, overused. "So, how many rooms do you have?"

"Two, if you don't count the bathroom. The bedroom's over there." He motioned toward a door painted lime green.

"Who lived here before you? Someone who was colorblind? I feel like I should put on my sunglasses."

"Yeah, the place needs work, all right. If I buy the paint, will you help me repaint it?"

She wanted to agree, but an alarm went off in her head. She reminded herself that she shouldn't spend too much time with Jeff, or she might find herself involved with him again. "I have to begin work on my school's play. I'm doing makeup."

He looked disappointed. "So maybe you can help me choose a color."

"White," she offered immediately. "It goes with anything."

After a minute of awkward silence, he jumped up. "I went to the grocery store and bought some stuff. I got you diet soda because I know you shouldn't drink the sugar stuff."

She disliked being reminded of her diabetes and

wasn't sure if she should be pleased for his thought-fulness. "I usually drink diet," she said, "because it cuts down on calories. Who wants to be fat?"

He returned from the shoebox-size kitchen with a glass of clear, bubbly pop and handed it to her. "Why do girls always think they're fat when they're not?"

"You know what they say—you can never be too rich or too thin." The glass was chipped, so she turned it before taking a sip.

"Are you really trying to lose weight? What about your diabetes?"

"Why the third degree? I didn't come here to be grilled." The reference to her health annoyed her.

"I'm just asking a question," Jeff said apologetically. "I have to think about my hemophilia before I do anything. I'm a bleeder and have to always take it into account."

"I'm careful, but I don't want to sit around gabbing about it." She was doubly glad no one at school knew, if this was the way people might treat her.

Jeff shrugged. "So how was the play with your dad?"

"*Cats* was good."

"And the rest of the 'date'?"

"We got through it."

He must have sensed her reluctance to discuss her feelings about her family, because he dropped the topic and asked, "What do you hear from Katie and Chelsea?"

"I talked to them just before you picked me up. Chelsea sounded good, scared though."

"Scared? She's come through the worst of it—the operation and all. Now all she has to do is start living."

Lacey sensed that it was going to be more difficult than that for their friend. "Chelsea's never been to a day of regular school all her life because of her heart condition."

"So what?"

"It's not easy to simply waltz into a big school and expect everybody to be your friend. She's starting at ground zero."

"You and Katie are her friends."

"But we live miles apart. I'm talking about the everyday variety."

Jeff grinned. "What kind of variety is that? Do they look different? Have special names?"

"Don't act dense. You know what I mean."

He reached out and fingered the tips of her hair. "Friends are friends. You can't sort them into categories."

"Sure you can. There are sometime friends and forever friends. Then there are Hi-how-are-you friends."

"I'll be any kind of friend you want," Jeff said softly.

She knew he wanted to be more than friends, yet there was no way she could have Jeff mingle with her crowd from school. He was good-looking all right, but he was sick. And he might spill the beans that she was imperfect in the health area too. It was a chance she didn't want to take. She pulled away, set the soda glass down on a Formica-topped table, and stood. "I really should be getting home. Thanks for showing me your apartment. It's nice, and I hope you have a great semester."

He stood beside her. "In other words, don't call you again."

"Don't make it sound as if I don't care about you. I told you already, I'm busy with school. It's nothing personal. Besides, once you get into classes, you're not going to want to hang with me. I'm a high school kid. You'll find some college girl."

"Will you keep in touch?"

"I'll call."

"I don't suppose we could seal it with a kiss, could we?"

In spite of herself, she felt the corners of her mouth twitch with a smile. There was no way she'd allow him to kiss her again. It might make her forget the reasons she didn't want him in her life. She held out her hand. "I'll let you kiss my ring."

"Always cool, calm, and collected, aren't you, Lacey?"

"It's part of my charm." She didn't dare let him know that the coolness was something she wore like a shield to keep out the things of life she couldn't deal with. And at the moment, she couldn't deal with Jeff McKensie, his crystal-clear green eyes and the way his grin made her heart beat like a runaway train.

"Take care of yourself, okay?" At the doorway, he paused.

"I always do."

"And call me if you need me."

She promised she would, although she silently told herself, *It'll never happen.* She didn't plan on needing anyone.

"Liar!" Lacey spat the word at her bathroom scale. The needle didn't mind her outburst. It stuck stubbornly to its claim. *Three pounds!* How could she have gained three pounds in less than a week?

She stepped off the scale and kicked it. The first rehearsal for the school play was today. Ms. Kasch, the drama teacher, had asked that everyone involved with the play attend the initial meeting, so that meant Todd would be there. And so would Monet, who'd signed up to paint sets at the last minute. And Monet was model-thin, while Lacey felt like a fat toad.

"I'm leaving for work," her mother called.

"See you tonight," Lacey returned.

Alone, she tugged on a pair of jeans and studied herself in the mirror. Her size-eleven jeans felt tight, and she hated the way her tummy strained the denim material. If she didn't do something drastic, she'd have to buy size thirteens. She shuddered over the thought.

Her stomach growled, reminding her that she *must* eat breakfast and get her insulin shot. In a foul mood, she went to the kitchen and jerked open the refrigerator door. She picked up an apple, made a face at it, and tossed it back into the refrigerator bin. She thought back to the time when she'd been diagnosed. As her islet cells had died off, and with them, her body's ability to produce insulin, she'd gotten thinner and thinner. Sick too, but right now all she thought about was the wonderful thinness.

Slowly, an idea formed in her head. If insufficient insulin had caused her to lose weight before, then why couldn't it work again? Not like the other day, when she'd forgotten her shot accidentally. Without any insulin, she'd had to go to the bathroom continuously, plus she'd felt pretty rotten. Omitting her insulin altogether might not be such a good idea. But what if she simply cut back on her dose? Give herself less than her doctor had prescribed? As long as she stayed out of ketoacidosis, she could drop weight effortlessly. Plus, the lower dose would help her avoid dreaded insulin reactions.

"Why didn't I think of this before?" She shut the refrigerator door and got out her insulin supplies. Carefully, she drew her normal amount of insulin into the syringe. *How much to cut back?* she wondered. Ten units? Fifteen? She settled on fifteen from her morning dose and ten from her evening dose. "If that's not enough, I'll increase the decrease."

She smiled over her clever wording. Yes, this was a perfect solution to her problem. She promised herself she'd eat less too, and pig out on vegetables and low-fat stuff. Confident she could strike a balance between lowering her insulin dose and shedding unwanted pounds, Lacey dabbed an antiseptic-soaked cotton ball on her abdomen, pinched up a layer of skin, and stuck the syringe into herself.

Feeling satisfied with her compromise, she properly disposed of the empty syringe, mixed up an instant breakfast milk shake in the blender, returned to her bedroom, and quickly finished dressing for school.

Five

"Wow, you sure do go to the bathroom a lot."

Terri's comment caused Lacey's cheeks to burn with embarrassment, yet she laughed and casually said, "I've always been this way. I think it's a genetic flaw."

"No matter," Terri said. "It's just that while you were gone, Ms. Kasch told us to hurry because we have to have this flat totally painted before we can leave."

Lacey groaned. It was already after six, and the particular flat the crew was working on was elaborate with detail. At the rate they were going, she'd be lucky to be home by eleven. "What about supper?" she asked.

"Maria and Gordon are making a hamburger run. Give them your order and some money."

Lacey hated the idea of loading up on fast food for another meal, but what else could she do? She had to eat.

"You've lost weight, haven't you?" Terri asked.

"A little. And it isn't easy to diet when my menu consists mainly of fat grams either."

"Tell me about it. This play is ruining my figure. I wish I had your willpower, Lacey. I just smell a chocolate milk shake and I gain. How do you do it?"

"I have my methods." In truth, she'd been juggling her insulin dosage for three weeks and she'd lost twelve pounds. Of course, going to the bathroom frequently and feeling sluggish and irritable were side effects she still was learning to tolerate.

"Methods for what?" The question came from Todd, who strolled toward them.

Lacey felt her pulse quicken. "Dieting. I thought you were rehearsing."

"Taking a break." He stopped in front of Lacey and allowed his gaze to roam her body. "Tell me about your method. It must be a good one, 'cause I think you have one fine body."

Terri snorted. "Get real, Todd. Cars have fine bodies. Girls are people. We often have fine minds."

"Excuse me for appreciating Lacey." Todd's tone wasn't kind.

Flattered by his attention but uncomfortable with the tension between Todd and Terri, Lacey interjected, "And I appreciate your appreciation . . . so how's the rehearsal coming along? Memorized your lines yet?"

"Not entirely. Maybe I could use some coaching." He eyed her again in a suggestive way.

Before she could respond, Monet came up and hooked her arm through Todd's. "I've been looking for you."

Todd turned toward the tall, willowy blonde, and Lacey felt as if she'd been shoved aside. "You found me," Todd said.

"And you're flirting with other girls. Honestly, Todd, what ever am I going to do with you?"

Lacey saw Terri roll her eyes and make a gagging noise.

"Since it's a dinner break," Todd said to Monet, "why don't I take you out for pizza?"

"Love to." Monet continued to hang on his arm.

Once they were out of earshot, Terri said, "That girl's so icky sweet, it's a wonder he doesn't catch diabetes from her."

"You can't catch it." The words were out of Lacey's mouth before she could stop them.

"Says who?"

Lacey would have given anything to take back her statement. How could she have been so stupid to blurt it out? "I—um—just read an article about it. Diabetes isn't contagious. It's sort of a hereditary thing."

"You mean like your bathroom problem?"

Fortunately, Terri grinned, so Lacey sidestepped the question by saying, "My real problem around here is Monet."

"She does have *moxie*, doesn't she? She comes right up and interrupts Todd's conversation with you and gets an invite to dinner while we have to settle for cardboard hamburgers. And pizza yet! He could afford to treat the whole cast to lobster, you know."

"What baffles me is how she never gets fat."

"She doesn't seem to pay calories much mind," Terri said in agreement. "I've seen this girl chow down. Once, she ate a whole quart of chocolate ice cream at one sitting. I wonder how she stays thin enough to land those modeling jobs."

Lacey felt a twinge of envy. Such a binge on so much sugar and fat would probably land her in the hospital—especially now that she was manipulating her insulin dose in order to run higher blood sugars to help eliminate weight. "A whole quart? You're kidding."

"I'm not kidding. And because it was chocolate, I almost wrestled the spoon out of her hand."

Lacey laughed. "I'll bet you'd eat that flat if I poured chocolate sauce on it."

"Please, I have my standards. I'd eat that flat only if it were *made* of chocolate."

Lacey slapped her palm against her forehead. "What was I thinking?"

Gordon pushed open the backstage door and called, "Chow's here."

"Oh, goody," Lacey sighed. "Another five thousand calories for only five bucks. What fun."

In minutes, the cast and stage crew gathered, sorted out their orders, and shuffled off into smaller groups to eat. Lacey and Terri settled in a far corner of the dusty backstage area, where they sat cross-legged on the bare floor. Lacey nibbled on her burger, which had already grown cold.

"Want some fries?" Terri asked.

Lacey peered into the unappetizing mound of french fries. "No thanks. I don't even want this." She tossed down the burger. "I should have gotten a salad."

"Rabbit food?" Terri made a face.

"Have you ever seen a plump bunny?"

"Get off the fat routine already. You look fine."

With a start, Lacey remembered her shot. That morning, she'd tucked her insulin and a syringe into her purse. *Good thing too*, she told herself. She'd didn't want to have to take a shot when she arrived home after eleven o'clock. "I have to hit the bathroom again," she said to Terri.

"Again?"

Lacey shrugged. "Nature calls."

"I'd say she was shouting at you, girl."

"Save my place," Lacey called over her shoulder as she dashed away. She found her purse where she'd stashed it in the prop room and hurried off to a bathroom in the farthest, darkest recesses of the theater.

Once inside a stall, she rummaged in her purse for her diabetic supplies. Her fingers fumbled with the syringe as she squinted in order to see the tiny demarcations along the barrel of the needle that aided in measuring out her correct dosage of insulin. She automatically backed off the dose by ten units and slid the sharp needle into her flesh.

She was putting things away in her purse when

she heard the bathroom door open. Lacey froze. She gripped the syringe tightly in her hand and pressed herself against the cold metal side of the stall. She heard someone go in the stall next to her. Lacey held her breath and felt sweat dripping down her back.

All at once it occurred to her that she had every right to be there in the bathroom, but she also realized that by making an appearance now after she'd been so quiet might seem weird to the other person. *Stay put*, she told herself. *Don't make any noise, and sneak out.*

Lacey heard the latch close on the adjacent stall and waited for the girl to make some noise so that she could escape undetected. What she heard next was the sounds of someone throwing up. She eased open the lock on her stall and crept out.

Now what am I supposed to do? Lacey wondered. From the sound of things, the girl was really sick. Maybe she should go and tell someone. Trembling, unable to decide whether to flee or help, Lacey stood in front of the locked stall door trying to make up her mind. Before she knew it, the awful sounds of retching stopped and the next thing she heard was the sound of the toilet being flushed. In a panic, Lacey stepped backward, but not before the stall door opened and Monet stepped out.

The two girls locked gazes, each shocked at seeing the other. Monet recovered first. "Well, what are you staring at? And why did you follow me in here?"

Monet's accusation angered Lacey. "Excuse me, but it's a public facility, isn't it? Who died and left you in charge of planet earth?"

Monet brushed past her. At the sink, she bent her head and rinsed her mouth under the faucet. Monet was shaking visibly. Her skin was the color of paste and covered with perspiration.

Watching her made Lacey remorseful over her cutting words and she asked, "Are you sick? Do you need some help?"

Monet straightened and caught Lacey's gaze in the mirror. "I'm perfectly fine."

"But I heard you being sick. You look ill."

Monet spun. "Oh, Lacey, grow up! I was purging."

"Purging?" The truth dawned on her slowly. "You mean you were forcing yourself to vomit? Why?"

Monet crossed her arms and leaned against the sink. "Because I ate pizza and drank beer. I can't eat that stuff day after day and stay thin. Who can?"

"Yeah. Who can?" *So that was Monet's secret!* She'd have never known if she hadn't caught her. Lacey found the truth unsettling.

"Everybody does it," Monet said. "It's the best way I know of to eat exactly what you want but never have it settle around the waist." She managed a tight smile that made her eyes look like bright, hard marbles. "But you're not going out there and blab it all over the set now, are you?"

"I'm not a gossip, Monet. I don't care what you do with your dinner."

Monet's expression reminded Lacey of a cornered cat. Suddenly, her eyes narrowed, then she arched one delicate brow and asked, "What's that in your hand? From here, it looks like a needle. Tell me, Lacey, are you doing drugs?"

Six

LACEY FELT COLOR drain from her face. She clutched the syringe so tightly that the tip of the needle jabbed her palm, making her wince. She felt blood trickle from the prick.

"I asked you a question?" Monet said, moving closer. "I mean, I'm not judging you if you are using. If that's your bag, your secret's safe with me. Just like I know my secret's safe with you."

"I don't do drugs," Lacey said, forming the words with precision.

"Then why the needle?"

For a moment, Lacey's mind went blank and panic rose in a wave. She couldn't tell Monet the truth. Not Monet. "I have allergies," she said, amazed at how easily the lie came to her. "I take shots to build up my resistance."

Monet looked disappointed in the explanation. "Well, maybe I believe you and maybe I don't."

"I don't care what you believe." Lacey slipped the syringe into her purse and went to the sink, where she rinsed off the line of blood made by the needle's tip.

"But you're still going to keep your mouth shut about me, aren't you? People will believe what I tell them about you. And if I say you're doing drugs . . ." Monet allowed the sentence to trail, implicit with innuendo.

"I told you I wouldn't say anything to anybody about your dinner-purging routine. I keep my word." She made eye contact in the mirror with Monet to emphasize her point.

"See that you do," Monet said, and swished out of the bathroom.

Lacey let the water run on her hands and watched them tremble. *Too close a call*, she told herself. All she needed was Monet spreading stories about her. Lacey sighed and stared absently into the mirror. She saw dark circles under her eyes. When had they cropped up? She *was* feeling tired. And hungry too. She dried her hands and on her way back to join Terri, she stopped at a vending machine and bought a package of peanut butter crackers and a diet cola.

Lacey worked alongside Terri until Ms. Kasch sent everybody home for the night. Exhausted, Lacey went to her car. Todd pulled alongside and asked, "Got a minute?"

She nodded, wishing she didn't feel so dragged out. He invited her into his sports car. "Where's your bird dog?" She climbed into the contoured front seat, the chilly February air reviving her.

"Monet had to leave earlier. Something about meeting her agent for breakfast in the morning. Besides, she's not my keeper, you know."

"Could have fooled me." Lacey watched Todd's face in the light of the mercury lamps of the parking lot.

"I choose who I want to see," he said. "And right now I want to see you."

Her heart tripped a beat, but she decided to play it cool. "So you're seeing me. Is it a thrill?"

He laughed outright. "It's a thrill." He reached over and toyed with a tendril of her blond hair. "Your hair feels like silk."

Her mouth went dry and she ran out of clever things to say. "Todd, what do you want?"

"I was thinking I'd like to take you out sometime. Would you say yes?"

"Ask me and see."

"How about Saturday night? There's a party at a house on South Beach. It should be a real blowout."

She would have preferred a simple movie date, a quiet evening of one on one. "I'll go with you."

He grinned. "I'll pick you up at nine."

They talked over a few more plans, then she got out of his car and into her own. Once he'd driven away, Lacey sat and stared out over the metallic hood of her car feeling . . . hollow. Somehow, she'd always thought that having Todd ask her out would be a red-letter moment, but now that it had happened, she felt deflated and let down.

Lacey wished she felt better physically because that would make her feel better emotionally. "You're just wiped out," she said aloud. Suddenly, an overwhelming urge to go to the bathroom hit her. Quickly, she shoved the car into gear and headed out of the parking lot, hoping that she could hold it until she got home.

"You looked pale and tired, Lacey. Maybe going to this party tonight isn't such a hot idea." Lacey's mother eyed her daughter speculatively. "And you look thinner too. I think you're overdoing things with school and the play."

To keep from screaming, Lacey took a deep breath. "Mom, I'm fine. I look pale because it's winter and haven't been out in the sun, I look thinner because I am thinner. I'm trying to knock off a few pounds before spring and bathing suits come back into fashion."

"Is that wise? I mean, you have discussed this with Uncle Nelson, haven't you?"

Lacey had not consulted her mother's brother, of course. He'd never approve of Lacey's juggling of her insulin doses, but she couldn't tell her mother. "I might have mentioned it on the phone." Lacey hated to lie, but she liked the way her body was looking and her clothes were fitting and didn't want to spoil it.

"Well, just so long as he knows what's going on." Lacey eyed the clock. They were standing in the kitchen, where the table was piled with one of her mother's work projects. Todd was late and Lacey kept wishing he'd hurry up and come for her. "I can handle my diabetes," she declared. "Haven't I been doing it for years?"

"It's a mystery to me why you even have diabetes," her mother groused. "I don't know for sure, of course, but I doubt it came from my side of the family."

Lacey ignored her mother's subtle swipe at her father. "I didn't wish it on myself, you know."

Her mother glanced up, surprise stamped on her face. "I didn't say that you did. Goodness, who would? I'm simply concerned about you and want to be certain you're taking good care of yourself."

"Well, don't be. It's my problem, and I'm handling it."

"You have an appointment next Friday with Uncle Nelson. His office called to remind us."

Inwardly, Lacey groaned. She couldn't go for her regular three-month checkup next Friday. Her uncle would discover what she was doing and make her stop. "I won't forget," Lacey told her mother, deciding that she'd call her uncle's office on Monday and reschedule the appointment for the following month. Surely by then she'd have lost all the weight she wanted.

Mercifully, the doorbell rang. "Todd's here." Lacey called, hurrying to the front door.

"Don't be too late," her mother called after her.

Lacey pretended not to hear her. She'd stay out as

late as she wanted. She was sick and tired of adults telling her what to do!

The party was in full swing when Lacey and Todd arrived at a soaring modern house of white stucco, glass block, and jutting decks of concrete set with Spanish tile. A live band blasted out the newest hits, and people crowded in rooms and on winding stone staircases. The back of the house faced the beach, where a partial moon glimmered down on a rolling surf. The night was cool but pleasant, almost balmy, heavy with the scent of salty surf.

"Have a beer," Todd yelled, thrusting a bottle into Lacey's hand. She didn't want it, but she didn't want to appear uncool either. She took a few deep swallows, trying to disguise her dislike of the bitter taste.

"Who's party is it?" she asked above the music.

"Don't know. I got an invite from a friend of my brother's. He's in college."

Lacey could tell that it was an older crowd. She didn't know a soul except Todd and missed the familiar faces of her high school friends. "Anybody else we know going to be here?"

"Not hardly." Todd grabbed her hand. "Let's go find something to eat. I'm hungry."

She wasn't, but she tagged along after him, dodging people. In the dining room, a glass-topped table stood laden with food. Chairs had been pushed against the wall and dark hardwood floors gleamed under a spectacular chandelier. Todd grabbed two plates and heaped them with food. "I can't eat all that," she said.

"Come on, this stuff's great. Don't be like Monet, always whining about calories."

Lacey stiffened. The last thing she wanted was to be compared negatively to Monet. "I can probably outeat you, buster," she quipped.

Todd grinned. "That's more like it."

The beer had gone to her head and the smell of the food was making her nauseated. She had to go to the bathroom too. Why hadn't she given herself a little more insulin before her date? She wouldn't be feeling so queasy, or thirsty.

"I'll be right back," she told Todd, and set her plate down. He gave her a questioning look. "I need to find the powder room," she explained, and hurried off.

She found the bathroom, then she decided to go outside and get some fresh air. She hoped it would clear her head and calm the queasiness. The night air was invigorating, and the music wasn't so blaring.

She gazed at the surf, then at the moon. "It almost looks like you could walk to the moon, doesn't it?" a voice said beside her.

She turned and stared dumbstruck at Jeff McKensie.

Seven

"**W**HAT ARE YOU doing here?" she asked as soon as she could find her voice.

"A frat brother dragged me." His gaze appraised her. "How about you? Isn't this a little out of your high school league?"

Miffed that he would remind her she was too young to fit in, she said in her frostiest tone, "My date brought me. I didn't know I needed your approval."

He threw up his hands and backed off. "Whoa! Don't go for the jugular. I'm surprised to see you, that's all."

"I didn't expect to meet anyone I knew, let anyone you," she said. "You took me by surprise too."

"So where's your date?" Jeff glanced about, but

the only other people on the terrace were couples in embraces.

"He went for something to eat."

"Since you're alone temporarily and since we seem to be the only people out here without our lips locked, how about going for a walk along the beach with me?"

"I shouldn't."

"Why? If your date snaps his fingers, do you have to jump?"

"I'm not anybody's lapdog. I just think it's a courtesy not to run off with another guy. Call me old-fashioned." Yet, as she spoke, she spied Todd through the glass doors dancing with a tall red-head.

"Then I'll walk by myself," Jeff said, starting down the steps.

She watched Todd and the redhead nuzzle each other's necks and felt jealousy, then anger. Why would Todd do such a thing? "Wait, I'll come with you," she told Jeff, losing any sense of loyalty toward Todd. "I've always liked the beach at night."

"Even if you have to see it with me?"

"That's not nice. I have nothing against you."

"You avoid me like the plague."

By now they were walking along the shoreline, dodging the softly rolling waves. "I tried to explain to you that it's nothing personal. Besides, by now I figured you'd be knee deep in girlfriends."

"Why would you think that?"

"Well, you're attractive and—" She interrupted

herself because she hadn't planned to tell him any such thing.

"Tell me more." He'd stopped walking and caught her arm.

"Don't let it go to your head."

"Wouldn't dream of it."

She could see his eyes sparkling in the moonlight, and she was furious with herself and at him for being able to get to her so quickly. "I'm going back to the house."

Jeff's hands traveled up her arms and took hold of her shoulders. She pulled against his insistent tug, and met resistance. "I keep thinking of this past summer, Lacey. I keep remembering the woods around Jenny House and the fireworks."

"The fireworks were great on the Fourth of July," she whispered, feeling snared by his gaze. Her heart hammered in her chest, and she felt powerless to move away from him.

"I wasn't thinking about those fireworks."

"What other ones were there?"

"These," he whispered, dipping his head downward.

When his mouth touched hers, Lacey felt transported to the woods of North Carolina. The scent of the sea faded. The sound of the surf receded. Her arms floated effortlessly around Jeff's neck, and a slow-melting fire flowed through her veins. She rose on tiptoe and gave herself to the kiss. To the sensations pulsing through her. His lips felt warm and strong, the kiss burning and fiery on her skin.

When it ended, she could feel him trembling.

She heard him take a deep breath as he leaned his forehead against hers. She could hardly breathe, and she was afraid to move, as if movement would shatter the magic world surrounding them like glass. "I didn't think lightning could strike the same place twice," he mumbled.

She hadn't thought so either. It wasn't supposed to be this way. She wasn't supposed to feel this way about him. But she did. Nothing had changed since the summer. He could rock her to the tips of her fingers and toes with a kiss. "It's only chemistry," she said. "I've heard about such things."

Jeff pulled away and looked deeply into her eyes. "It's more than chemistry, and you know it."

Lacey felt overwhelmed by emotion. Suddenly she wanted to cry, to weep uncontrollably, and she didn't know why. "No," she insisted. "This kind of stuff happens only in romance novels."

"It's because I'm sick, isn't it?" he said flatly.

His question so caught her off guard that she stammered, "I—I don't k-know what—"

Jeff stuck his hands in his pockets and stepped aside. A wave splashed over the tops of Lacey's shoes, soaking her feet and leaving them chilled. "I know the signs because it's happened to me before," Jeff said. "I like a girl and then she finds out I'm a bleeder. Instant turnoff. But you knew from the beginning, Lacey, so I thought it didn't matter to you. But it does matter, doesn't it?"

She went hot and cold all over. It was as if he'd shone a light into some secret part of her heart and something dark and ugly had crawled out. She *had* rejected Jeff because she didn't want a sick boy-friend. She'd said as much to Katie at Jenny House. "It's any sickness, Jeff. It's mine too. I hate it all. I know it's not your fault, but it's not mine either."

"I'll bet no one at your school knows you're a diabetic."

She said nothing.

"I'm right, aren't I?"

"It's none of your business."

"You know, Lacey, you're the person who won't accept that you have a disease. Why is that?"

She whirled on him. "How can you ask me that when you've just admitted that girls drop you once they discover you're a bleeder? You of all people should understand why I keep my little secret."

"I don't like being a hemophiliac, but it's what I am. I can't be responsible for girls who can't handle it. Who can't see past the illness and accept *me*. I do know that I have some pretty incredible friends who know about my problem and who care in spite of it. Give people a chance, Lacey. They just might pleasantly surprise you."

"I'm not that way," she said. "I can't go around telling people that I'm sick. I'm *not* sick. I manage my diabetes just fine."

"Get over it. If they're really your friends, it won't matter. And if it does matter, then they aren't the kind of friends you need."

"I'm not going to stand here debating this with you. I'm handling my life just fine and I don't need any pointers from you. I don't want *anything* to mess things up for me this year."

"Such as me," Jeff added with finality. "I get the picture."

Emotionally, she felt wrung out. Her blood sugar was high too, she could feel the semiqueasiness in her stomach and an ache in her head. Much too high. "I should have never taken this little walk with you, Jeff. Whenever we're together, we end up fighting." *Just like my parents*, she thought but didn't voice.

"I'll walk you back to the house and see that you hook up with Mr. Wonderful."

"Todd's not Mr. Wonderful. He's just a guy." A guy who didn't care, who'd never care about her, the way Jeff did, the inner voice reminded her.

Once they returned to the party, they discovered Todd guzzling beer with a group of guys, oblivious of Lacey's presence. Lacey stared in dismay. She certainly didn't want to be in a car with a drunk driver.

"The guy's too smashed to take you home," Jeff told her. "I'll take you."

"You don't have to—"

"What will you do? Hitchhike? Call a cab?"

Knowing she didn't have many choices, Lacey nodded. "All right."

"Are you going to tell him you're leaving?"

She looked at Todd, at the beer oozing down his chin, at his arm draped around the shoulder of another girl. "He won't notice. Let's go."

During the drive home across the causeway spanning Biscayne Bay, she and Jeff didn't speak. Once he parked in her driveway, she reached for the car door handle. He pulled her hand away. "Don't be so skittish, Lacey. I'll walk around and let you out. You're not my prisoner."

When he took her to her front door, she stood for a moment, shifting awkwardly from foot to foot. "Thanks for the ride. I did need one."

"I hope you heard some of the things I said to you tonight."

"I know what I'm doing, Jeff. What's right for you isn't right for me."

"And I don't mean anything to you, do I?"

"You're my friend."

"Big deal."

She couldn't back down now. She couldn't let him know how she really felt about him. It would ruin everything. "We were friends at Jenny House. We're friends now. What's wrong with friends?"

He shook his head. "Because I don't want to be your friend. I want more than that. Time is short for me, Lacey. I never know from day to day if I'll have a bleeding episode, or if I do, if I'll make it through. You're wrong if you think I'll settle for only being your friend."

"*You're* wrong. We *are* friends. If you go to the hospital, I'll visit you. All you have to do is call me."

He pinned her with a hard stare. "You do whatever you want. You always do anyway. Like I said, I'm not holding you prisoner."

She watched him disappear into his car in the moonlight. *You're not my prisoner*, he'd told her. She felt tears brim in her eyes. He was wrong about that.

Eight

⁓

"Where'd you run off to Saturday night?"

The question came from Todd, who'd cornered Lacey in the prop room Monday after school and before the start of play rehearsal.

"I'm surprised you noticed," Lacey said breezily, hoping to disguise the sense of ambivalence she felt toward him. She was still attracted to him, but she didn't want him to think he could walk all over her.

"I noticed all right." He caught her arm. "And I don't appreciate it. When I take a girl out, I expect her to stay with me and go home with me. Someone told me you left with another guy."

"And I expected you to stay with me at the party. I saw you hanging all over some redhead at one point, and I figured I'd been replaced."

"Well, you figured wrong. I was just dancing with

her. But so what? You didn't have any right to leave with somebody else."

Lacey gave him a frosty stare and pulled her arm free of his grip. Her knees were shaking, but she sensed that Todd was used to getting his way with girls and she didn't want to simply be another trophy for him. "So sue me. I went home with a guy I already knew because you were *blotto* and I don't ride in cars with *blotto* drivers."

"I had a few drinks. Maybe if you had a few, you wouldn't be so uptight all the time. What's the matter with you anyway? Don't you know how to have a good time?"

There was plenty she could say about why she didn't drink—everything from "It's illegal" to "I don't like the taste." Naturally, the foremost reason was her diabetes, and she'd *never* volunteer that information. "Why do you think it's impossible to have a good time unless you're drunk?" she countered.

"I didn't know you were such a loser. I'm really sorry I bothered with you. Next time, I'll pick a girl who wants to have fun."

She watched him walk away and realized that being dumped by Todd meant being placed on the outside of the hallowed circle of Miami High's in crowd. She'd wanted to be a part of it for so long!

"You did the right thing, you know." Terri stood beside her, watching Todd exit the prop room.

"How long have you been listening? Don't you know it's rude to eavesdrop?" Lacey was angry. Angry at having Terri see her humiliated, angry at Todd for holding out the carrot of popularity and then snatching it back.

"Why do you care about that turkey? Leave him to Monet; they deserve each other."

"It's not that easy." Lacey wished Terri would drop it, because there was no explaining to her why Todd and his world appealed to her. She wasn't sure she even knew *why*.

"I know!" Terri said brightly. "You need a pick-me-up. Something to take your mind off that jerk. Come with me."

"Where?"

"It'll be a surprise."

"We can't just up and leave. Ms. Kasch is expecting us to work on the set." Lacey didn't need much persuading. She wanted to be out of there too. Away from Todd's contemptuous gaze.

"We've been here every day for weeks and she allows three unexcused absences. This counts as one." Terri grabbed Lacey's hand and pulled her toward the outside stage door which she flung open. "Look. It's spring. Blue skies. Bright sun. Smell that air. We shouldn't be locked up in that smelly, dark theater."

Lacey allowed Terri to take her to a parked car. "Nice wheels," Lacey said, surveying the sleek black sports car.

"My brother Ramon's. He let me drive it today and I promised to deliver it to him at his job." Terri shut Lacey inside, got into the driver's seat, and started the engine. "I know just what you need to get rid of the blue funk Todd put you in."

"What's that?"

"A feeding frenzy." Terri shoved the car into gear and took off.

"Isn't that something sharks do?"

"And people who need to transcend the blahs. I do it all the time."

Eating was the *last* thing Lacey wanted to do. "Sorry, I'm low on cash."

"No problem. Ramon is the manager of one of the hippest restaurants in Coconut Grove. We can eat ourselves into a stupor and never be charged a dime."

"Oh, I don't think—"

"I'm telling you, this place is really an experience. After we dine on everything on the menu, it's off to Bailey's Ice Cream Parlor. Imagine . . . double chocolate fudge ice cream smothered with hot fudge, marshmallow sauce, whipped cream, nuts, cherries. It's like dying and going to heaven."

Lacey was speechless. She couldn't eat that stuff. "But my diet—"

"Begin again tomorrow. Tonight it's food heaven." Terri turned to her and grinned. The wind whipped her dark hair, and overhead the bright blue sky streaked past. "My treat," she said with a beaming smile. "How can you say no to that?"

Lacey couldn't. Not when Terri was trying so hard. Not when she suddenly felt ravenous. She thought about her insulin shot and how she'd planned to give it to herself secretly in the bathroom. She decided that it would be too risky to sneak off while she was with Terri; better to forget it altogether tonight. What harm could it do? She was already running high blood sugars to lose weight, so skipping one shot at this stage shouldn't be too bad. "Does Ramon's restaurant serve lobster?" Lacey asked. "I have a weakness for lobster dripping with melted butter."

"Lobster and steak," Terri said. "It's called Surf and Turf." She picked up the receiver of the car phone. "I'll just call and tell him to start our steaks right now."

Lacey laughed and felt excitement bubbling up inside her. Terri was right. She needed to get out and have fun. And eating was fun. She'd been on this stupid diet much too long and it was time to take a break. "I like mine medium rare," she said above the sound of the traffic. "With mushrooms smothered in butter."

The restaurant was everything Terri had promised. Lacey had never been in such a fancy place, or pigged out on such delicious food. She ate until she thought she would burst. "Save room for Bailey's," Terri cautioned.

"I don't think I can eat another bite," Lacey groaned.

"Don't tell me that. This is a lesson in gluttony, and I expect you to be a good student."

Ramon checked on them and insisted they take home the remains of their dinner in doggie bags. Lacey thanked him while pushing aside the pangs of guilt for eating such a mountain of food.

In the parking lot Terri traded cars and she and

Lacey headed down the quaint streets of the Grove. There was no persuading Terri to return to the play rehearsal, so against her will and better judgment Lacey ended up at the ice cream parlor facing an impossible mound of a gooey sundae made with three different kinds of chocolate ice cream.

"It's called Death by Chocolate," Terri said, digging her spoon into her sundae. "Don't be shy, eat up."

Lacey took a tentative bite and savored the sweet, sugary flavor. Although sweets were not forbidden to her as a diabetic, they were something that had to be planned for and worked carefully into her menu. Sweets by themselves could not cause diabetes, but real sugar did cause elevated blood sugars and needed more insulin to metabolize properly. Still, she loved the taste of desserts and found the huge bowl of ice cream irresistible. "I'll bet I've gained ten pounds tonight."

"You needed the break," Terri said, popping a plump red cherry into her mouth. "So tell me, who's your best friend?"

Immediately, Katie came to mind, then Chelsea, but to mention them might open up an area of discussion Lacey wanted to avoid. Her friends were sick, or had been sick, and that might lead Terri to wonder why Lacey knew them in the first place. "I guess you are after this."

"Good choice. I had a best friend, Sharon, but she moved away. That was last year. We write, but it's not the same, is it?"

"Not really," Lacey said, rooting through her sundae for an elusive cherry and hoping Terri didn't ask any more questions. When your best and dearest friends were sick girls, it was difficult to talk about them.

"Sharon wants me to come see her this summer. She lives in Houston. But I need to get a job. What will you do this summer?"

Lacey thought about Jenny House, about the promise she, Katie, Chelsea, and Jillian had made to one another about meeting again at Amanda's memorial on top of the mountain. In her mind's eye she saw the stick tepee she'd constructed, the photograph fluttering in the breeze, the diamond stud earring Jillian had fastened to the picture. But Jillian was dead. And Chelsea's transplanted heart could reject. For that matter, so could Katie's.

"Excuse me. Earth to Lacey." Terri was rapping the side of her water glass with her spoon. Lacey started. "You checked out on me," Terri added. "Is everything all right?"

"Sure," Lacey insisted. "My brain wandered. Probably too much food and it didn't know how to react."

"Well, believe it or not, even I'm on food overload." Terri stuck her spoon into the gloppy remains of her ice cream. "But I feel better. At least my emotions do. And you? Wasn't I right? Didn't you need to eat your way out of that run-in with Todd? I'll bet you haven't thought about him once all evening."

It was true. She'd completely forgotten about Todd. But memories of her friends crowded in and disturbed her. They were doomed. All of them. No matter how well they did with their transplanted organs, their lifespans were shortened. So was Jeff's.

Lacey felt sick to her stomach. The overload of food was beginning to take its toll. She was thirsty —horribly thirsty. And she had to go to the bathroom. She went at the ice cream parlor, then again the second she told Terri good night and thanks and got inside her house.

Fortunately, she was alone. Her Mother had left a note saying she'd gone out with friends. Lacey paced the floor, furious with herself for the eating binge. Terri had no way of understanding what this pigout was doing to her body. She felt dizzy and weak and her throat burned with unquenchable thirst. A dull headache throbbed behind her eyes. She didn't know how to manipulate her insulin to take care of the excess. If only she hadn't eaten all that sugar and fat! If only she could get rid of it all.

Then, in the darkness of the hallway, she remembered Monet in the theater bathroom. *"I was purging,"* she'd said. Of course. Vomiting was one quick, sure way to rid herself of the food. "I've got to do it," Lacey told herself in the dark.

Without another thought, she hurried into the bathroom and shut the door.

Nine

~◆~

AFTER A FEW weeks, Lacey was amazed at how incredibly simple it became to make herself throw up. For the first time in years, she was able to eat anything she wanted, anytime she wanted—just so long as she could rid her stomach of its contents before the food could actually be digested. And the freedom to eat and not gain weight made the job of juggling her insulin much simpler.

She stopped checking her blood sugars altogether. "Why worry about it?" she told herself. Purging herself of unwanted food would keep her blood sugar level, wouldn't it? Besides, things at school had picked up. Instead of blowing her off, Todd was paying a lot more attention to her. She wasn't sure why, but she was glad of it.

Play rehearsals had moved into their final week

and Lacey was responsible for overseeing makeup, her favorite part of theater and drama. She was applying thick stage makeup to Todd's face, her back to the dressing mirror, when he asked, "Did you just paint your fingernails?"

"No, why do you ask?"

"You smell like that stuff girls use when they do their nails."

She held her hands under his nose. "See, no polish."

He shrugged. "I'll be glad when this play's over. It's taken over my life."

Lacey considered the completion of the play a mixed blessing. On one hand, it was exciting and fun, and she was with Todd every night. On the other, she was absolutely exhausted. Getting up in the mornings was a struggle. She fought off a deadened sleep that seemed leechlike, sucking her energy before she even opened her eyes.

"Ms. Kasch wants the cast onstage." Terri said as she stuck her head through the open door.

"But I'm not finished," Lacey explained. Her fingers felt thick and sluggish, unresponsive to her commands to hurry.

"It's only a dress rehearsal," Todd said, pulling the towel that protected off the collar of his clothing and tossing it on the dressing room floor.

Lacey bent over to retrieve it and was struck by a wave of dizziness.

"You all right?" Terri asked, taking hold of Lacey's arm to steady her. Todd had already left the room.

"Fine." Lacey offered a shaky smile while thinking, *It can't be an insulin reaction.* She hadn't had a reaction from low blood sugar in ages.

"You look sort of flushed," Terri said. "You coming down with the flu or something?"

"You sound like my mother. She's been on my case because she thinks I'm too thin." Lacey rolled her eyes. "As if anyone can be *too* thin."

Terri tapped her finger, thoughtfully studying Lacey. "You have lost plenty of weight. But I've seen you eat and you don't exactly pick at your food."

"I have a healthy appetite."

"You have healthy kidneys," Terri joked. "I've seen how often you exercise them."

Lacey allowed Terri to laugh at her expense. If only Terri knew *how* active her kidneys were these days. Lacey felt as if she spent half her life in the bathroom.

After rehearsal, Lacey headed for her car, looking forward to going home and diving into her bed. Todd caught up with her in the parking lot, looping his arms around her waist and nuzzling her neck. "What's the hurry?"

"I'm wiped out and I still have a test to study for," she explained.

"But I need a kiss."

She turned her mouth upward and felt his lips press hard against hers. She only wished she didn't feel so drained so that she could have enjoyed it more. But then, she never had enjoyed Todd's kisses as much as Jeff's—Lacey put the brakes on the turn her thoughts had taken and slid her arms around

Todd's neck. *Enjoy!* she told herself. Hadn't this been what she wanted since September?

Driving home that night, Lacey noticed that her vision was blurring. "Oh, great. I'll probably have to get glasses," she complained aloud to her reflection in the rearview mirror. She blinked and rubbed her tired eyes. "A little sleep. All I need is a little sleep."

She stepped inside the front door, only to be confronted by her mother. "I've been waiting to talk to you," her mother said.

"Can it wait until tomorrow, Mom? I'm really tired."

"No, it cannot wait."

Lacey gritted her teeth and tossed her books and purse onto the catch-all bench along one wall of the foyer. "What wrong?"

"Uncle Nelson's office called today and left a message on the answering machine. The nurse said that you'd missed your appointment—*again.*" Her mother looked angry.

Lacey groaned. She'd rescheduled her appointment twice and had totally forgotten to do it again. "I forgot," she explained. "I'll call and make another one tomorrow."

"I talked to Nelson tonight. He said he hasn't seen you for over six months. I asked him if it was important, and he almost bit my head off. He said, 'You bet it's important.' He fussed at me, Lacey. My own brother criticized *me.* As if it were my fault you weren't going in for your checkups. I've always let you handle your diabetes. You said you could. But now I discover that you're not managing it at all."

Lacey was in no mood to argue. "The play is over this weekend. Two more rehearsals and four performances. I think I can put off my doctor's appointment for a few more days. Cut me some slack, Mom. I've got a million things on my mind and I don't need to be nagged about some stupid appointment." Lacey was breathing hard when she finished her speech, but it worked, because her mother muttered something about "being responsible" and "get it done," then stalked off.

Lacey went into her bedroom and sprawled across her bed. Both her head and stomach hurt. Maybe Terri was right. Perhaps she was coming down with the flu. The high-tech buzz of her telephone pulled her out of a groggy stupor. Lacey fumbled with the receiver.

"You sound fuzzy. Did I wake you?" It was Katie's voice.

Lacey glanced at the clock. It was only ten-thirty, too early to feel so wiped out. "I just got in from play practice. How are you doing? What's up?"

"My frustration level is topped out." Lacey waited patiently for Katie to explain, willing herself to focus on her friend's words. Katie was too good a friend to put off, especially since they didn't talk on the phone very often. "I want to go away to college, but my folks and Josh are really putting the pressure on me to stay home and go to Michigan in the fall."

"It's a top-ten school. Would that be so horrible?"

"But I want to go away. I've lived here all my life, and except for going on a few vacations and spending the summer at Jenny House, I never get out of Ann Arbor!"

"But your heart—"

Katie let out a little shriek. "Not you too? You're the one person I expected to support me. My transplant's doing great. Why shouldn't I go off to college?"

Lacey was ashamed of mentioning Katie's health —the one thing she hated most for people to mention to her. "Sorry. I lost my head for a minute. Of course you should go away to college. Where do you want to go?"

"That's the problem. No one's offered me a scholarship yet. I could use my Wish money for tuition, but I'm still holding out for the possibility of scholarship money. Plus an athletic scholarship would make my parents much more inclined to let me go off. Which brings me to why I called."

"You want a contribution from me to the Katie O'Roark scholarship fund?"

"Very funny. No, guess where the high school national track competitions are being held this year?" Katie didn't wait for Lacey's guess. "Miami," she cried. "And even though the season's just started up here, our girls track team is seeded number one in the state. If we win the state, then we come to Florida."

"Somehow I have no doubt you'll be down here. When's the big event?"

"Not till May."

Lacey felt a slight letdown. It was mid-March. She wished she could see Katie sooner. All the things that were happening to her seemed too complicated to discuss over the phone, and she'd never find the time or energy to write it down in a letter. "Well, I hope you get to come. You know if you do, I'll be in the stands cheering for you."

"I'm writing Jeff and telling him too. I know he's transferred to the U of M. I guess you've made a point of not seeing him." Because Lacey paused before answering, Katie added, "I thought as much. I still think he cares about you, Lace—although I can't figure why. You treat him like a nonperson."

"Don't nag. I have my reasons." Lacey quickly hurried to talk about the play and the fun she was having at being part of Todd's exclusive crowd. "He may ask me to the prom," she finished.

"Garrison's asked me to our senior dance, but I know Josh expects me to go with him."

"And you should. Josh is your guy."

Katie mumbled something about "ruts" and "same old routines," but Lacey was having difficulty paying attention. "I'll call you after opening night," Katie said. "You can tell me how the play went. And how brilliant a job you did on the makeup."

Lacey said good-bye and headed immediately to the bathroom. There, a wave of nausea swept over her that was so intense, Lacey began to retch and vomit into the toilet bowl without even having to force herself to do it. *I have to get better*, she told herself. Too many things were going her way, and she didn't want to get sick and blow it all now. *Hang on!* Katie used to tell Amanda. "Hang on," Lacey repeated to her flushed-looking face in the bathroom mirror.

Ten

THE PLAY OPENED on Thursday night and the buzz of excitement backstage ran through the cast and crew like an electric current. Lacey moved from person to person applying stage makeup to members of the cast, feeling as if she were moving through a thick, clinging fog. Her mouth felt dry and parched, and no amount of water seemed to slacken her thirst. On top of the thirst, she also felt nauseated.

"I could use a little help here," Todd snapped.

"You're not the only person going onstage tonight," Terri countered as if she sensed Lacey was having trouble keeping up.

"I wasn't talking to you, Terri."

Lacey stepped between them, saying, "I'll handle it." She quickly drew lines on his forehead, a technique to age him for his role.

"After the performance tonight, I want to take you out," Todd said, eyeing Terri. "Someplace private."

To Todd, "private" meant being alone with no danger of interruption. "We'll see," Lacey said, knowing she wasn't in a mood to be with him. "Tomorrow night would be better."

"It's not better for me."

She chalked up his bad temper to first-night stage jitters. "We'll talk about it after the play," she insisted.

Just then Monet swept backstage. Her dress was short and black and her blond hair fell past her shoulders in a sleek veil. She looked tall and slim and beautiful. "I thought I'd give you a kiss for good luck," she told Todd.

He pulled her into his arms and kissed her. Lacey felt the old familiar twinge of jealousy. Without a word she turned and walked out of the dressing room. Terri met her in the bustling hallway. "I don't know why you let that guy pull your chain," Terri grumbled.

Lacey shrugged listlessly. "I don't know either. Right now I'm too tired to care."

"Boy, you don't look like you feel real good."

"Maybe I do have the flu."

"Too bad you can't pass it along to Mr. Wonderful."

Mr. Wonderful. That was the sarcastic term Jeff had used for Todd. Suddenly, a deep yearning sprang up inside Lacey to see Jeff again. Not only to see him, but to be with him, talk to him. He understood what it was like to feel bad physically, and Lacey knew that was part of her problem. She had no one to talk to about her health, and she was scared about what was happening to her. Somewhere over the past couple of months she'd lost control of her life, and now she felt helpless to turn the tide that was threatening to engulf her.

"Curtain going up!" the stage manager shouted.

Instantly, the hallway cleared and everybody scrambled for their places. "Want to go out front and watch?" Terri asked.

"No. I want to sneak into one of the dressing rooms and fall asleep," Lacey confessed.

Terri hesitated for only a minute. "I'll go with you."

Secluded in one of the rooms, Lacey tugged off the smock she'd donned to protect her clothes from makeup smears. As she pulled the smock over her head, her shirt slid upward, exposing her bare midriff. "Jeez, Lacey. I can count every one of your ribs," Terri exclaimed, her brown eyes wide with shock.

Intrigued, Lacey tossed the smock across a chair and stepped up to the vanity counter and its bank of mirrors. She held up her shirt and saw exactly what Terri had meant. Her ribs stood out in relief on her torso. Her skin looked stretched and papery thin, and her stomach seemed almost concave.

"You look like a war orphan," Terri declared. "Maybe you should lay off that diet."

Lacey felt alarmed over her appearance too, but she pulled her shirt down and tucked it into the loose-fitting waistband of her jeans. "Maybe I should see if Monet's agent could use another model." She tried to make light of the situation.

"Maybe you should eat something."

"I'm not hungry. All I need is a drink of water."

"I'll get it for you. You don't look as if you can make it to the water fountain and back."

Lacey sat down heavily in a chair. "All right, I'll let you." In truth, she was grateful. Exhaustion was consuming her, and she felt dizzy and light-headed. Nausea passed through her in waves, and for a moment she was terrified that she might start throwing up. Something was wrong with her. Terribly wrong. She didn't have the strength to move. Her arms and legs had stopped obeying her commands and felt like lead weights. Her head flopped against the back of the chair.

"Here's your water."

Terri's voice seemed to be coming through a tunnel. Lacey struggled to answer.

"Lacey, are you all right?" Terri's voice sounded anxious, but try as she might, Lacey couldn't form words. Her breath grew rapid and shallow, and she became so dizzy that she thought she might float right off the chair.

"What's wrong? Lacey, please say something!" Terri's voice sounded frightened, but no matter how hard she struggled, Lacey couldn't respond.

"I'm getting help," Terri cried.

Lacey wanted to stop her because she didn't want to cause a scene. She just needed a little sleep. Sounds came to Lacey in riffs, like waves breaking on a shore. Darkness came too, segments where she lost contact with the sounds and the glaring lights of the vanity mirrors. She gasped for breath, then lapsed into the quiet shadows while the sounds of running feet, adult voices, and excited babbling scraped against her eardrums.

"What's wrong with her?"

"I think she's unconscious."

"She's sick. Really sick."

"Lacey. Lacey. Say something."

"Call an ambulance."

"Better call her mother too."

Her mother would be angry, Lacey wanted to tell them. But suddenly, she wanted her mother with her. And her dad too. But they were divorced. And warring.

Hands lifted her, placed her onto a couch, and covered her with a blanket. In the distance, a telephone rang. *Maybe Katie was calling,* Lacey thought. But no, Katie wouldn't call the theater. She heard running feet and metallic noises. She again felt herself lifted, this time by men's hands onto something that was cushioned, a bed with cool sheets. Someone pried open her eyelid and shone a bright light straight into her eye. She tried to turn away.

"Start an IV," a man's voice said. "Saline. She's dehydrated."

"Is she dying?"

"Clear out of the way," the man's voice commanded.

Someone else was crying. Terri?

The bed started to move, and then Lacey was outside in the night air and the metal clacking stopped as she was rolled through an open door inside a vehicle. Red lights reflected off people's faces, giving them an eerie, nightmarelike quality. Lacey allowed herself to drift away once more.

"Lacey! Lacey honey . . . it's Uncle Nelson. Can you hear me?"

When she could focus, she realized that she was no longer in the theater or the vehicle. Uncle Nelson's face was right above her, and she wanted to ask him why he'd come to see her. All around her she was aware of people moving and of a sharp antiseptic odor.

"You're in the emergency room, Lacey," her uncle told her.

She drifted off hearing him command, "I want her up in ICU. *Stat.*"

She was aware that her bed was rolling again, and when it stopped moving, more hands lifted her onto yet another bed. She heard murmuring, felt needles pricking the backs of her hands and round sticky pads being stuck to her chest. She heard the sounds of machines blipping and humming and Uncle Nelson's voice coming from far away.

"It's your diabetes, Lacey. You're in keto and I don't know why, but I'll find out. Hold on."

But she couldn't hold on. It was too much effort.

"Your parents are here and they'll be in just as soon as I can get you settled."

Her parents? Together? Lacey felt a numbing sensation that pulled like quicksand, or an undertow, sucking her into a sea of darkness. She fought against it, panicky, like a drowning swimmer. But the numbness crept upward, seizing her legs, then her arms, and finally her mind. The last thing she remembered was the bleep of a machine and the cold, quiet terror of falling headlong into a dark and bottomless pit.

Eleven

LACEY FELT DRUGGED, mired down, weighted by tentacles of sleep she couldn't quite shake loose from. She recognized the comings and goings of people— nurses, her uncle, her parents. She even recalled hearing her mother crying, which surprised her. Her mother never cried. Not even when Lacey's father had moved out.

She heard her father call her "Daddy's girl." He hadn't called her that since she was ten. She heard Uncle Nelson giving instructions to nurses, and she was aware of tubes being changed that had been inserted into parts of her body. The one down her throat hurt whenever it was removed, and she was relieved when they didn't put it back.

Yet Lacey had no sense of time as she drifted. The artificial lights were always dim, never indicating if it was day or night outside her glass cubicle. When there were no people around, the machines kept her company and their mechanical rhythms kept diligent vigil, sometimes comforting her, other times frightening her. She would drift into wakefulness, hear their beeping and wonder, *Where are the people? Why aren't there any people?*

Finally, however, Lacey was able to free herself from the snakelike arms of the unnatural sleep that held her and floated into complete wakefulness. A bright light was shining in her eyes, and her uncle's voice said, "Welcome back."

"Where—?" Her voice was wobbly and strangesounding to her ears. And her throat hurt.

"ICU," her uncle answered. "You've been here two full days and three nights.

The news shocked. Over two days of her life were missing and all she knew about them were pale glimpses of reality. "What's wrong? My throat—"

"The soreness is due to the gastro tube we put in because you were vomiting. You've been in a diabetic coma. We've got you stabilized, but I still don't know *why* it happened. There are no secondary infections, nothing medical that might have caused it. I'm baffled, Lacey. So I thought that as soon as you woke up, I'd ask you why. Any ideas how this could have happened?"

She didn't want or need a lecture from him, so she avoided a direct answer. She said, "I'm tired."

"Your parents will want to see you," he said, not forcing the issue of her collapse. "They've been here day and night and they're worried sick."

"You mean they've stayed in the same room together without fighting?"

A smile curved Uncle Nelson's lips. "Extraordinary, huh? Nevertheless, they've put aside their differences for now. I'll send them in. Later, I'll have you transferred to a private room."

"I am going to be okay, aren't I?"

He eyed her with a cool medical calm that made her glance away. She was scared, but didn't want to show it.

"We've got to get to the root of this problem. Diabetes is serious and can cause severe complications over time. But you've been a diabetic for years, Lacey. You know the basic facts."

She knew, but had glossed over them. Complications were for "other people," not sixteen-year-old girls such as herself. "You can send my parents in," she told her uncle.

Her mother and father looked ready to explode with relief when they entered the cubicle. "Oh, baby! We've been so worried about you." Her mother's eyes shone with unshed tears.

"Lacey, it's wonderful to see you alert. How do you feel?" Her dad needed a shave, further evidence of his concern. He was *always* clean-shaven.

"How did this happen, Lacey?" her mother wanted to know. "I thought you were doing so well. It's because you skipped your appointments, isn't it? I should have kept a closer check on you. I blame myself."

Lacey was in no mood to listen to her mother's

self-recriminations. "Nagging me wouldn't have made a difference, Mom."

"But why? How could this have happened?"

"No need to bombard her, Sandra," Lacey's father said.

"Alan, I'm not bombarding her. I'm simply asking what went wrong. How could she have allowed herself to lose total control of her illness."

"Maybe she didn't lose control. Maybe something else is going on."

Listening to them made Lacey's stomach constrict. "Has anybody from school called?" she asked, interrupting their argument.

Her parents turned toward her. "A girl named Terri," her mother said.

"No one else?"

"Your friend Katie called twice from Michigan. She's pretty upset and wants you to call her as soon as you're able."

"Uncle Nelson says I'll be moved out of ICU later today. I'll call Katie and Terri then. And anybody else who's asking about me. I'll be going home soon anyway."

Her parents exchanged glances. "Hasn't your uncle talked to you?"

"About what?"

"About your hospitalization."

Lacey experienced a sensation of cold foreboding. "What about it?"

"You're going to be here awhile," her father said. "Maybe a couple of weeks. They want you to undergo evaluation by a diabetes specialty team. To determine why this happened to you. And to make sure it doesn't happen again."

"What do you mean, I can't get out of here for a couple of weeks?" The words tumbled out Lacey's mouth the instant her uncle walked into her private room that evening. "I have to go to school. I can't hang around the hospital."

Her uncle put on his best doctor expression and sat down on the side of her bed. "I can't let you out until I know exactly what triggered your DKA."

"I didn't plan to go into keto, you know."

"Lacey, anyone who's monitoring their blood sugar regularly, giving their insulin shots, and maintaining an exercise program shouldn't go into keto. At the very least, you should have smelled the buildup of acetone on your own breath."

She recalled Todd asking her if she'd painted her fingernails. He had smelled the acetone and she'd dismissed his observation. *How stupid!* She told her uncle nothing because she knew he was goading her into confessing that she'd blown it.

"You've lost a lot of weight," Uncle Nelson observed. "Were you dieting?"

"I was counting calories," she admitted. "But keto made me lose weight."

"And your blood sugar testing didn't warn you of elevated glucose levels?"

"So I wasn't testing too regularly. I let it slip by on me."

He arched an eyebrow. "That's an understatement."

"Well, I hate being in the hospital and I don't see why I have to stay here. I can go to school and come in for regular visits."

"Like you did these past six months?"

Her cheeks reddened and she felt anger welling up inside her. She wanted to jerk out the IV and march out the door. "I hate being here," she restated. "I hate all this equipment. I feel like a freak."

He fingered the line attached to a small machine parked next to her bed. "This is an insulin infusion pump, and until we get you completely balanced, I want you on it. Think of it as a vacation from your twice-daily injections."

Her gaze followed the line that was threaded into her arm, where a needle was inserted under her skin and taped in place. "Some vacation."

"There are worse machines to be attached to," he said enigmatically.

"What's this stuff about a team I have to see?" She changed the subject because she didn't want a lecture on the dire consequences of diabetes.

"An approach we use now for newly diagnosed patients. A patient sees not only the physician, but also a nurse educator, a dietician, an exercise therapist and"—he took a breath—"a counselor."

She stiffened at the last word. "You mean like a shrink?"

"A psychologist who specializes in family counseling."

"Haven't you heard, Uncle Nelson? The Duvals are no longer a family."

"Nevertheless, all of you are going to be talking to Dr. Rosenberg."

"Are you sure this doctor wants to be in the same room with Mom and Dad? It could be hazardous to his health."

"*You're* the one who's important," Uncle Nelson declared. "*They're* the ones who have to learn to work together for *your* benefit."

"That'll be the day."

Uncle Nelson patted her hand. "I have other patients to see, Lacey, but I'll be in tomorrow morning after I take a look at the readings from your blood work. I'll be bringing the team with me for you to meet. They're a good crew. You'll like them."

I doubt it, Lacey thought, watching him exit her room. She hunkered down in the bed with an overwhelming urge to cry.

She might have started crying too, but a hesitant knocking sounded on her door. "It's open," she called.

The door opened and Terri poked her head inside the room. "Are you up for company? Or are you in quarantine or something?"

Twelve

⁓

LACEY FELT HER spirits lift as if attached to a helium balloon. She beamed Terri a smile. "Come in. Come sit down. Tell me what's happening? How'd the play go? How is everybody?"

Terri crossed to the bed cautiously, peering hard at Lacey from beneath the brim of a funky hat. "Hey, slow down. One question at a time. First of all, are you going to be okay?"

"I'm fine."

Terri eyed the IV line and insulin infusion pump skeptically. "You sure?"

"These contraptions will be gone in a few days."

"What happened to you?" Terri edged down into a chair positioned alongside the bed. "I won't lie. We were all totally freaked when you collapsed at the theater."

Lacey's face stung with embarrassment. There was no keeping the truth hidden about her being a diabetic any longer. "I caused a real scene, huh?"

"The play stopped and everything. An ambulance came and took you away. We were all pretty scared."

Lacey groaned and buried her face in her hands. It was worse than she thought. She'd never live down the humiliation. "This is so gross," she mumbled into her hands. She looked up. "Everybody thinks I'm a total freak, don't they?"

"They think you're *ill*." Terri's tone was empathetic. "Tell me, what's going on? All your mother would tell me was that your diabetes was out of control. I didn't know you *had* diabetes. Why didn't you ever say anything to me about it?"

"Nobody knows," Lacey said miserably. "I hate having it."

"But I thought we were friends." Terri looked hurt.

"I don't see any reason to dump on a friend."

"All the times you kept going to the bathroom and when you wouldn't eat junk food—it was because of your diabetes, wasn't it?"

"I wanted to lose weight," Lacey insisted stubbornly.

"And I had to drag you out for an eating binge." Terri rolled her eyes. "I'm really sorry."

"Don't blame yourself. I had fun that night."

"Do you have to stick yourself with a needle every day?" Terri wasn't even trying to mask her wide-eyed curiosity.

"Twice a day. But let's not talk about it."

Terri began chattering. "I went to the school library. I looked up diabetes in the encyclopedia. It was pretty interesting. Diabetes is one of the oldest diseases in recorded history. The ancient Greeks wrote about it. *Diabetes mellitus* means 'sweet urine.' The article explained that people who have it can go blind, or lose limbs 'cause of nerve damage, or have kidney failure. I don't want that to happen to you."

"It won't," Lacey said without much bravado. "I just got a little messed up, but I'll be back in control and on top of this in no time."

"I sure hope so."

"But enough about me," Lacey insisted. "How'd the play go?"

"After the ambulance left with you on Thursday night, Ms. Kasch told us to go on with the play, but the cast never really got into it."

Lacey hated hearing that. "So was it a total flop because of me?"

"No . . . just subdued. It went better Friday and Saturday nights. We struck the set today after school."

"And—um—the cast party? How'd it go?" Lacey was supposed to have gone with Todd. He'd asked her in his usual offhanded manner one night following a dress rehearsal.

"I didn't stay very long. But you know me, I'm not much of a party girl."

Lacey thought it maddening the way Terri wasn't telling her what she wanted to know. "I guess Todd took Monet," Lacey said, half hoping Terri would say "no way."

"Yeah, he brought Monet. I told you he was pond scum."

"He's free to date other girls." Lacey defended him even though she was hurt. Her mother had never mentioned whether he'd even called to check on her. She supposed that he hadn't.

Terri fiddled with the strap of her purse lying across her lap. "In school today, Monet was bragging that Todd asked her to the prom."

The news washed fresh waves of humiliation over Lacey. He wasn't giving Lacey the chance of a comeback; he simply substituted another girl to fill her place. And every person at school who'd seen them together would know the same thing: Lacey had been unceremoniously dumped. "I guess this means I can cancel my dress fitting at Neiman-Marcus," Lacey said breezily.

Terri smiled ruefully. "I'm glad you're not letting this get you down. I wasn't sure how you'd take the news."

Lacey was upset, but not so much by Todd's betrayal as by the sense that she was losing something she'd worked hard to have—a feeling of normalcy and belonging. "I hate hearing the news," she confessed. "But it doesn't surprise me."

"I'm sorry you even cared for Todd. You're more than he deserves." From the hallway, a voice on the PA system announced that visiting hours were over. Terri rose. "They're throwing me out."

"Will you come back?"

"Sure. How long will you be cooped up in here?"

Lacey remembered what her uncle had told her about an extended stay for counseling. "I'm not positive."

"Well, you won't miss too much school. Spring break and Easter's coming."

Lacey grimaced. "I hate thinking about spending vacation time in this place."

"I'll check out the beaches for you. The college crowds have already started bombarding Florida. 'Course, it would be more fun to do this together." Terri shrugged. "Maybe next time."

Depression descended on Lacey once more after Terri was gone. They should be out on the beaches together. *She* should be the one planning on attending the prom with Todd instead of Monet. She should be thinking of having fun instead of facing counselors and dieticians. Diabetes had ruined her life.

When her phone rang, she offered a listless hello.

"Lacey! Is this really you? I've been frantic worrying about you!" Katie's voice exclaimed.

"I'm a loser, Katie. Now everybody at school will know what a loser I am." Lacey explained her circumstances, venting all her frustration and hostility into Katie's ear.

"You can't help it if you're sick," Katie said patiently. "Diabetes isn't exactly the plague, you know. Maybe things won't be that grim at school. Lots of kids and teachers were sympathetic toward me when they learned about my heart problem."

"Is that what you wanted?" Lacey found the courage to say. "Pity? Not me. I don't want everybody talking about me behind my back. I was in sixth grade when I was first diagnosed, and I can remember when I came back to school after being in the hospital, a group of kids used to whisper about me. Some of them called me needle freak and junkie. It was awful."

"That was years ago, Lacey. You're in high school now. Don't you think kids might have matured a little since then?"

"No," Lacey said, sniffing. She told Katie what Terri had revealed about Todd. "So they haven't matured, Katie," she finished. "They've just figured out ways to be more cruel."

Katie quietly but firmly answered, "Listen to me, Lacey Duval. You can't blame Todd's behavior on your being sick—he's probably selfish and obnoxious no matter what. He doesn't sound like much of a loss. Besides, you've always told me he never turned you on the way Jeff did anyway."

"That has nothing to do with it."

"It has everything to do with it. You can't blame your diabetes for everything that goes wrong in your life."

Lacey stiffened. "Well, the last thing I expected from you was a lecture."

"Well, you need one." Katie now sounded impatient.

"No, I don't. I need a friend."

"I've always been your friend, Lacey. Chelsea and Amanda . . . Jeff too. And let's not forget Jillian. She liked you, and we had to practically bludgeon you to allow her to visit Mandy's memorial. Lots of people care about you, Lacey, but you have some stupid idea in your head about what's 'real' and 'normal.' Stop feeling sorry for yourself. You drive everybody away who tries to get close to you, and that's not fair."

"I'm so glad you told me what my problems are. Thanks for the enlightenment. I'm in the hospital, you know. I have a right to feel sorry for myself."

"Well, I'd prefer you start taking care of yourself instead of always looking for a way out of it. You've got a disease, Lacey. Stop pretending that you don't."

"And I'd prefer it if you'd lose my phone number. Permanently. The one thing I don't need is friends like you."

Lacey slammed the receiver down so hard that the phone skidded off the table. It lay on the floor in a tangled heap, sending out a mournful dial tone. "Who needs you, Katie O'Roark," she spat out through clenched teeth. Tears filled her eyes and began to flow. Furiously, she wiped them away. But it was like trying to stop a breech in a dam with a toothpick.

She needed Katie. Desperately. Katie was the best friend Lacey had ever known. And she'd just driven her away. With her mean mouth and hateful words, Lacey had slammed the door on their friendship forever.

She curled up into a ball and tugged the bed covers over her head, but the IV line in her hand prevented her from blocking out all the light in the room. The lights in the hallway dimmed. Lacey felt utterly and completely alone. Her sobs poured out, soaking her pillow.

Her uncle had done her no favor by rushing her to ICU and saving her life. He should have let her die. Dying would be better than this terrible burning pain in her heart. From the floor, the dial tone from the overturned phone turned into an intermittent whine that pierced her eardrums like the wail of a terrified child.

Thirteen

Lacey gazed up at the faces of the team of diabetes professionals surrounding her bed, and although her uncle introduced each member, she barely paid attention. A young woman named Sue, a dietician, said, "You know, learning to eat right doesn't mean giving up all the things you love and never tasting them again. It simply means planning. You can eat practically anything you want, just so long as you plan for it."

Of course, Lacey knew that much. "I don't have much of an appetite now," she said. "And I'm not interested in gaining back all the weight I lost."

"You don't have to gain back most of it," Sue said. "But when a patient goes DKA, she loses more than unwanted pounds. She loses muscle mass and vital nutrients. We've got to put those back, and naturally, weight gain will happen. But it's a healthy weight gain. We'll design an exercise program for you."

"I hate exercise."

"Me too," Sue said with a smile. "But everybody needs it. Even people without diabetes. You don't have to be a jock, but you do need an exercise routine."

Lacey thought of Katie, athletic to the core. The memory of their fight the night before caused fresh pain. She flashed Sue a hostile look. The woman was young and tall, slim and fit. Her hair was dark brown and hung in a French braid, her eyes brown and lively. "And I suppose you're on the hospital's softball team, bowling team, golf team, and every other team they have. How would you know what it's like to have to stop in the middle of everything that's happening and give yourself a stupid insulin shot? I've always had to sneak off at sleepovers and play rehearsals and measure out my insulin. What fun."

"I know what you mean because I've done it for years," Sue said. "I've been a diabetic since I was fifteen."

The news stopped Lacey's sarcastic tirade cold.

Uncle Nelson intervened. "You'll see everybody again this afternoon. Along with a private session with Dr. Rosenberg. But for right now, I want to take you for a little ride." He pulled a wheelchair to the side of Lacey's bed.

"I'm not going anywhere in that thing."

"Yes, you are," Uncle Nelson said firmly. "While

you're here, I'm in charge, and besides, I'm bigger than you, so get into the chair and don't give me any lip." He softened his tough talk with a broad smile and a wink.

Grudgingly, she got into the chair and waited while her insulin pump and IV pole were adjusted to travel with her. It was humiliating being wheeled down the hall followed by the apparatus of her condition. She still didn't feel good physically and wondered if she ever would feel good again. How could things have gone so wrong over the past few months? And when would she be able to resume a normal life?

Her uncle rode down with her in the elevator, wheeled her down a hall with signs reading RENAL UNIT, and into a room with several machines that stood beside chairs that resembled recliners. A person sat in each chair while lines from the machines snaked down his or her body and disappeared into a tube protruded from arms. One person was calmly reading, another was dozing, and one woman was busy knitting. The clack of her needles could be heard above the hum of the machines.

"Am I supposed to be impressed?" Lacey asked, feeling a coldness form inside her.

"This is the dialysis unit." Her uncle ignored her bad temper. "These people come in three times a week for four or five hours a day and have their blood shuttled through these machines to cleanse it of toxins and impurities. Their kidneys don't work, and without dialysis, they'd die."

"So what's your point?"

Uncle Nelson crouched in front of her chair and looked her in the eye. "Forty to fifty percent of all type-one diabetics—that's the type of diabetes you have—suffer from kidney disease. It may take fifteen or twenty years to develop, but nevertheless, once a diabetic's kidneys fail, he has only two options: dialysis or transplantation."

She listened to him, all the while watching the patients in the room. The machines looked grotesque to her, like giant birds of prey hulking beside beds, with gauges for eyes and tubes for beaks. Hours had to be spent hooked up to them. Hours of everyday life that should have been spent doing other things, fun things.

Uncle Nelson gestured toward the room. "This unit is for hemodialysis—it cleans the bloodstream. Often, diabetics do better on CAPD, continuous ambulatory peritineal dialysis.

"You do this kind at home. You have a catheter inserted into your abdominal cavity"—he touched her stomach area—"and then dialysis fluid is put in through the catheter's opening, where it sits for six hours attracting toxins and then is drained and replaced with fresh fluid."

She thought the procedure so horrific that she could barely imagine it. She'd be attached to an IV line for a quarter of the day, 365 days a year while the fluid did the job of failed kidneys. "If you're trying to scare me, you are," Lacey said, holding his gaze with hers.

"I want to scare you, Lacey. I want you to understand the reality of your disease. You're my niece

and I love you. I don't want this to be your future. It
saves many lives and is extremely important, but I
hope you won't have to use the machines to save
your life."

"I don't want it either."

"That's why it's important that you take care of
yourself."

"But it could happen anyway, couldn't it? Fifty
percent is a high number. There aren't any guarantees." Her hands were shaking, so she kept them
folded tightly in her lap.

"No guarantees," he said. "But studies do show
that the more tightly you control your blood sugar,
the better able you can manage and postpone the
side effects."

She edged her gaze away from his. "I take care of
myself."

He took her by the arms. "Lacey, you were
brought into the emergency room in DKA. That
couldn't have happened unless there was something else going on in your body, like a massive
infection or other illness." He paused. "Or if you'd
stopped your insulin shots."

"I was taking my shots," she said stubbornly.

He scrutinized her carefully. "When I examined
you, I saw that your throat and upper esophagus
looked irritated, consistent with a patient who'd
been vomiting. That's why I ran tests to determine
if you had food poisoning or a stomach bacterial
disorder. You didn't."

Her heart began to pound. He was getting close
to something she didn't want discovered. Her purg-

ing shouldn't have had anything to do with her problem. She had been careful to not do it after every meal, only just when she'd eaten too much of the wrong things. "I don't know what you want me to say," she said. "I was giving myself my shots."

He ducked his head and took a deep breath, then stood. "If you won't be honest with me, please come clean with Dr. Rosenberg. We've got to get to the bottom of this, and I won't let you go home until we do."

Lacey slept in her room until it was time to meet with Dr. Rosenberg. One of the nurses took her to his office in the wheelchair, chattering all the way and singing the doctor's praises. Still, she was prepared to dislike him. She didn't want to talk to a shrink and she didn't want to have him digging around inside her head for details about her psyche. She realized now that she'd made a mistake in trying to diet by juggling her insulin and purging. Why couldn't she simply put the past behind her and start all over?

Dr. Rosenberg was a short man with round features and jovial eyes. He reminded her more of a department store Santa Claus than a doctor. His office had an unkempt quality with stacks of papers and books on every surface, including the floor. "Sorry about the mess," he said after introductions. "I'm moving into the new wing of the Diabetes Research Institute, and housecleaning is a chore."

"My uncle's told me about the institute. It's just for diabetes research, isn't it?"

Dr. Rosenberg raised the blinds on the window, and she could see a glass and concrete building rising in the near distance, windows gleaming in the bright Miami sun. "It's the culmination of years of work and fund-raising," Dr. Rosenberg said. "The only one of its kind actually. A facility dedicated to finding a cure for diabetes while treating patients with the latest and best therapies available.

"If you want, I'll take you on a tour. We're dedicating the building in a big ceremony this fall. But some of us will be setting up shop before then. The finishing touches are being put on the place now."

"I don't think so," Lacey said. "I'm not much interested in buildings or diabetes."

He lowered the blinds and rolled his office chair in front of her, where he sat and offered a smile. "But you've had diabetes for several years. Don't you want to know what we're doing to cure it?"

"I just want out of here."

"I've met your parents," Dr. Rosenberg said, changing the subject.

"Then that explains the real reason your office is such a mess. Did they start throwing things?"

Dr. Rosenberg smiled knowingly. "They may not like each other, Lacey, but they love you very much."

"Sure. I'm the glue that held them together, all right."

"Do you blame yourself for their divorce?"

"Do we have to talk about this?"

"You should talk about it with someone. Your health is in jeopardy."

"Well, I don't feel responsible for my parents' divorce and right now I'm tired and I want to go back to my room." Her voice had risen as she spoke.

"Very well." Dr. Rosenberg rang for a nurse. "But will you come back tomorrow? I'm seeing your mother, then your father, in two separate meetings. I'd like to see you again too."

Of course she didn't want to, but she knew her uncle was expecting it. And she also felt that if she focused on talking about her family, then maybe she wouldn't have to fess up to her gross mismanagement of her diabetes. "I'll come," she told Dr. Rosenberg.

She was tired and drained, but back in her room she couldn't sleep. TV was boring and her vision kept blurring when she tried to read. Terri was in school. Katie wasn't talking to her. Todd was a lost cause. Lacey felt alone and cut off. Then she thought of the one person in the world whom she wanted to see and talk to.

With trembling fingers, Lacey picked up the phone and asked information to look up Jeff McKensie's phone number for her.

Fourteen

❧

"ARE YOU SURE you're all right?"

The anxious expression on Jeff's face as he asked his question stirred Lacey's heart. She'd caught him between classes at his apartment when she'd called and he'd come within the hour. He looked wonderful, so familiar and caring that all she wanted to do was throw her arms around his neck and hold tight. But she didn't because she knew how mean she'd treated him in the past. He probably didn't want anything to do with her and had come only out of pity.

"I'm not all right," she told him, admitting for the first time how bad the week had been for her. "I'm feeling sick and I don't have any energy. And I hate being attached to these things." She raised her arms. The lines from the IV and insulin pump dangled.

Jeff eased himself onto the bed, carefully pushed the plastic tubing aside, and slipped his arms around her. She felt his hands against the soft cotton of her gown, and a tingle shot through her. She slid her arms as best she could around him and laid her cheek against his chest. Enveloped in his arms, snuggled against his warm, broad chest, Lacey closed her eyes and gave in to the swelling dam of tears clogging her throat.

He let her cry, all the while stroking her long hair and rocking her tenderly. "It's okay, baby," he murmured into her ear. "Everything's going to be fine . . . I'm here now."

"I've made a mess of my life, Jeff," she sobbed. "I've gone and screwed things up really bad."

"The doctors will straighten you out—"

She interrupted. "It's not just my health. It's everything. I—I had a terrible fight with Katie. And everybody at school knows about me now. And Todd . . . well, he's never even called once to check on me."

At the mention of Todd's name, she felt Jeff stiffen. She hugged him all the tighter. She heard him ask, "Is that why you called me? To mourn your boyfriend?"

She pushed back and stared up at him, barely able to focus through the shimmering flood of tears. How could she explain what the loss of Todd meant to her? "*Todd* isn't important to me. It was never *him* that I wanted. Don't you see? Nobody has to take shots except me. Nobody has to plan for every little morsel of food that goes into their mouths except me. Have you ever had an insulin reaction in front of your friends? I have. It's awful. I feel like an outsider. I've told you before, I hate being sick, Jeff. Nothing's changed."

· He touched his forehead to hers and took a slow breath. "I hate being sick too. It isn't easy sitting on the sidelines all your life. When I was a kid I couldn't play hard because I might start to bleed. And when I did have a bleeding episode, I'd end up in the hospital getting a transfusion. When the AIDS epidemic came along, I watched a friend die because he got a transfusion of tainted blood."

Lacey gasped. "But you—"

"They do special screening of the blood now. Something like that doesn't happen these days, but still I have to be careful about my everyday life." He took her by the shoulders and, holding her gently, riveted his gaze into hers. "And don't think you're the only person to be rejected because another person couldn't handle dealing with an illness. Sometimes a girl thinks she can adjust to having a hemophiliac for a boyfriend, but when it comes down to it, she can't.

"Back in Colorado, when I was a junior in high school, my girl walked into my hospital room, pulled off a ring I'd given her, and dropped it on my chest while I was still getting my blood transfusion. Talk about feeling like a loser."

Lacey could see the hurt etched in his face. But she understood how fear could have made the girl do such a thing—she found it scary to care for someone who might suddenly die. "People are scared of taking on something they don't understand," Lacey tried to explain.

"Then they should *ask*," he countered. "They should make an effort to understand. I never made demands on anybody. I learned early on that it's one day at a time and nobody gets guarantees. I've had a perfectly healthy friend get killed in a car wreck. There was nothing wrong with him like there was wrong with me, but he's dead and I'm still alive."

"Life's not fair," Lacey said, feeling a tremor of anger.

"True. So what do we do about it? Check out of life before it deals us a nasty blow? If I'd done that, I'd never have gotten out of my basinet."

The image of him as a tiny baby made her smile. She asked, "But why did we have to have something wrong with us in the first place? Why did I get diabetes? It's screwed up my life."

Jeff toyed with a long strand of her hair. "Diabetes screwed up your life. My hemophilia screwed up mine. Nobody knows why. But one thing's for sure. You can't get even with your disease by ignoring it, or fooling around with it. It's meaner than you, Lacey."

He gave a quick smile when she reacted to his assessment of her. "And don't deny it. You can be short-tempered and mean as a snake. For crying out loud, there's not a nicer, kinder person in the world than Katie O'Roark, and you tell me you've had a blow-up with her. I mean it takes real talent to alienate a person like Katie."

She knew he was right. Her fight with Katie had been all Lacey's fault. All because she refused to face the facts of her life, as Katie had urged so many times. "I blew it, all right."

"I'll say." Jeff tweaked her chin playfully, then returned his hand to the strand of hair. "Somehow, you've got to work out a truce between you and diabetes. A peaceful coexistence, 'cause you're both living in the same body. Don't let it push *you* out. And don't give up any territory you don't have to give up."

Hearing him, seeing the earnestness of his face as he spoke, helped Lacey grasp something she'd never honestly considered. She, Lacey Duval, was at war with an old and ancient enemy—an illness that led to death. Diabetes could, and would, kill her. It had no respect for people. "Either I control it or it controls me," she said. "That's what you're telling me, aren't you?"

"You got it. Asking why won't change it. Even *knowing* why won't change it. It's here. It's alive and well. And until medical science comes up with a solution to get rid of it, it's sticking around."

Her loathing for her diabetes took on a new dimension as she grasped fully what Jeff was saying. Her illness was a part of her and there was nothing she could do to separate herself from its clutches. All she could ever hope to do is control it, make it do *her* will instead of her doing *its* will. Her eyes began to brim with fresh tears as reality sank in. "There's no magic to make it go away."

Jeff lifted her chin with his forefinger. "No magic."

She thought of the long road ahead of her. Of all the learning and adjusting, of all the food balancing and blood testing and insulin shots in her future. For though she'd been a diabetic for years, she'd never truly accepted it. She'd done only what was necessary to get by. And judging by her recent diagnosis of keto, she'd not done what was necessary very well.

"Will you come visit me while I get on top of this?" Her heart hammered as she asked. He owed her nothing and she'd done nothing to encourage him. To the contrary, she'd all but driven him away.

"I'll come visit you." His gaze looked guarded. "But don't jack me around, Lacey. I'm not going to be your buddy in the hospital only to have you run off to be with Todd when you get out."

"It won't happen. I told you, Todd and I are through."

"The world's full of Todds. Guys who get exactly what they want whenever they want because a girl has an idea that he's cool or in. I've played this hot and cold game before with you."

"When?"

"Last summer. And at that party a few months ago."

She felt color creep up her neck and cheeks. "I was angry with Todd at that party. I've learned some things since then."

"Like what?" His eyes were intense.

"I know *what's* important. *Who's* important." Memories flashed through her mind—the faces of Amanda, Jillian, Chelsea, Katie, Terri—and of the portrait of Jenny Crawford. These were the people who'd made a difference in her life.

"Am I important, Lacey?"

She reached out and pressed the tips of her fingers against his mouth. "Yes. Very much so."

She thought he might kiss her, but he did not. Instead, he stood and traced his thumb along the side of her cheek. "We'll see. I won't go jumping in with both feet this time. It hurts too much if I don't have something soft to land on."

He backed toward the door. "The ball's in your court now. Let's see what kind of a player you are. I'll see you tomorrow, Lacey."

She watched him leave, unable to think of a single thing to say to let him know she was accepting his challenge.

Fifteen

⤳

"WHAT ARE YOU up to, niece? Is this some kind of a trick or something?"

Lacey innocently gazed up at her uncle Nelson's face. "What do you mean?" She'd raised the top of her bed so that she was sitting upright. Her history book was open and she was reading the assignment Terri had brought from her teacher the night before.

"According to the diabetes team, you've been the picture of cooperation these past three days. You listen to every word from the dietician, you've worked with the exercise therapist, even Dr. Rosenberg says you've opened up with him. What's going on?"

Lacey offered her uncle a sweet smile. "Why, Uncle Nelson, don't you trust me? You told me you wouldn't let me out of this place unless I started learning how to manage my diabetes properly. I'm learning."

He ignored her smile and frowned sternly. "This isn't a game, Lacey. Don't go putting us on and then slip back into your old habits once you check out."

"Honest, I'm trying. I don't want to be sick like this again. It's no fun."

He came closer to her bedside. "I hope you mean what you're saying. Now that we've removed you from the insulin pump and put you back into the routine of injections, you'll have to monitor your blood glucose more closely than ever before after you return home."

"I'm testing four times a day and writing down the results in my log book like a good girl. Besides, I like being unhooked and free to wave my arms." To emphasis her point, she flapped her arms in an imitation of a bird.

He studied her chart. "You still don't look great on your lab reports. Your blood chemistry isn't straightened out yet, and I'm not sure what caused you to go sour."

She shrugged, unable to talk to him about how bad she'd blown it. She'd gained weight since her hospitalization, and at first she'd panicked, but Sue had assured her the gain was healthy and necessary. "I'm *trying*, Uncle Nelson. Please believe me."

He nodded and flipped her chart closed. "By the way, I've been meaning to tell you, I like that young man of yours—that Jeff. He's a nice kid. He's got his head screwed on straight." Lacey had introduced them when her uncle had come in for a visit and Jeff had been with her.

"My fellow? Where do you come up with these terms?"

"What should I call him?"

"He's not my fellow. He's a friend." She told him of meeting Jeff at Jenny House and of how he'd transferred to the University of Miami in January. Hesitantly, she added that he was a hemophiliac.

"Tough break," Uncle Nelson said. "But I still like him. And I think he's been a good influence on you. In fact, that whole Jenny House experience seemed good for you. Why did you lose it when you got home and back in school?"

"I guess I got sidetracked."

Her uncle squeezed her shoulder. "Well, I hope you're back on track for good now."

Her mother entered the room and Lacey felt an automatic tightening in her stomach. So far, her mother hadn't lectured her or bombarded her with dumb questions, and Lacey didn't want a confrontation now. Yet, when Uncle Nelson left, her mother pulled up a chair and said, "Lacey, we need to talk."

"If you're going to yell at me—"

"I'm not going to yell at you."

Lacey sighed and closed her book. "Look, I know you're disappointed in me. I know I was in charge of handling my diabetes and I let you down."

"You almost died, Lacey." Her mother's voice sounded teary. She sniffed and held up her hand.

"Wait. That's not how I want to start. You know I've been talking to Dr. Rosenberg."

"So have I."

"He's helped me see some things I wasn't aware of before."

"Like what?"

Her mother laced her fingers together and placed her folded hands in her lap. "You weren't the only one who had trouble accepting your diagnosis of diabetes when you were eleven. At the time, I thought I did, but deep down I was pretty shaken up by it. You were my only child and you were perfect and beautiful and charming."

"Oh, Mom . . ." Lacey felt flustered hearing her mother's opinion of her looks and personality.

"And until that time, you were healthy," her mother continued. "I just couldn't believe it. And I couldn't believe that I had somehow contributed to the gene pool that had made you sick."

"But you said that you and Dad couldn't trace it to either side of our family."

"That's true, but it had to come from somewhere. From one . . . or both of us." She was choosing her words carefully, and Lacey could tell that the effort was difficult for her. "If your father and I had never married, then most likely you would not have had the genes for diabetes. You would be well. You would have a normal life without the threat of blindness or kidney disease—all the side effects that go along with diabetes."

Her mother was feeling guilty! At fault for passing along flawed genes to her only child. At first,

Lacey thought her mother was merely feeling sorry for herself, but watching her as she battled with her emotions made Lacey pause. She'd never once thought what it must have been like for her parents when they'd heard the news of her initial diagnosis. Obviously, it had been shattering.

"I don't blame you and Daddy for my diabetes. And if you hadn't married each other, then I wouldn't be *me*, would I?"

"That's exactly what Dr. Rosenberg said too. But it still bothers me."

"Are you sorry you ever had me?"

Her mother reached over and grabbed Lacey's hand. "Never think such a thing. I love you and these past few days have been a nightmare. You were in critical condition and Nelson was very worried. He was totally honest with us. When I think how close I came to losing you . . ."

Lacey felt her own heart trip a beat. Had she truly been that close to dying? "I didn't mean to worry you or Dad. And I'll be more careful in the future."

"That's another thing. I know I haven't been the best at helping you manage your diabetes these past few years."

"It was my job."

"It was *our* job. Dr. Rosenberg says that some parents completely take over their child's illness, managing every aspect, worrying every time there's an elevated blood sugar reading, making their child so dependent and fearful that she can't function in the real world."

"You and Dad never did *that*."

"No. I became the other kind of parent. I decided it was best to let you shoulder the whole thing."

"You used to give me some of my shots. When I was younger . . . I remember."

"And I hated it. I couldn't wait until you took over the whole business and I didn't have to deal with it. Your father and I used to fight about it."

"You did?"

"He'd fuss at me for shirking my duty and I'd fire back that he completely ignored his role in your management. His idea of dealing with it was to dictate orders that I was supposed to follow like an obedient soldier."

"He never did any of the day-to-day stuff," Lacey admitted, remembering how their battles often revolved around words like "responsibility" and "lack of caring." She recalled her denial to Dr. Rosenberg that she felt responsible for her parents' divorce. "Is that why you divorced? Was it because of me?"

Her mother shook her head. "No. You and your diabetes often became the battleground, but our problems went far deeper than that."

Lacey wasn't convinced. It seemed as if they'd argued for years about one thing or another; she was sorry that her diabetes had been one more area of constant friction. "But you're divorced now," she said. "And I'm sixteen and I still have to be in charge of my diabetes."

Lacey watched a cascade of emotions cross her mother's face. "That's what Dr. Rosenberg said too."

"He's on my side?" Lacey was surprised. She had secretly wondered if the doctors would put her firmly under her mother's thumb like a naughty child.

"He warned me—us, your father too—that it was still *your* diabetes and that just because you'd blown it didn't make you any less responsible for it."

Lacey didn't know what to say. She half wanted, half loathed getting the total responsibility back.

"Dr. Rosenberg said there's a world of difference between inquiring and nagging. So I won't nag you about testing or appointments," her mother said. "I *will* ask you how you're feeling and what Uncle Nelson said during your checkups."

"That sounds fair."

"And I'll do a better job with dinnertime. I know I've been focused on the divorce and my job and haven't put a good dinner on the table every night for us."

"I can cook," Lacey declared. "I know how—but it would be nice to have you eat with me."

"The new Diabetes Research Institute will have special cooking classes once it opens. Maybe we could take a class together," her mother offered.

Lacey wasn't enamored of the idea, but she told her mother it would be okay.

A nurse came into the room to remind Lacey of her appointment with Dr. Rosenberg. "I'm glad we talked," her mother said as Lacey was ready to start down the hall to Dr. Rosenberg's office.

Lacey admitted that she was glad too. It was the first time for as long as she could remember that she and her mother had actually talked without recriminations or lectures. "Will you see Dr. Rosenberg again?"

"Yes. He's helping me immensely. I know your father's seeing him too."

"Then it's a family affair," Lacey observed. "Sort of ironic, don't you think? Now that we're not a family anymore."

As the nurse walked her down the hall, Lacey knew that if Dr. Rosenberg could bring about change in her mother, then perhaps it was time that she came clean with him. If she did, however, would he recommend that her diabetes management be taken away from her? She decided it was a chance she'd have to take if she was ever going to get out of the hospital and back into a normal life.

With heart pounding, she went inside his office.

Sixteen

LACEY TOLD DR. Rosenberg about the talk with her mother.

"You sound pleased," he said, steepling his fingers together and peering at her through them.

"I guess I am. I mean, all we usually do is yell at each other. Or, rather, she yells and I tune her out."

"It's not an uncommon pattern for parents and teenagers."

"So if you're making progress with Mom, how's it going with my father?"

"I haven't seen him as frequently. He's been bogged down in his business."

Lacey felt a twinge of disappointment.

"But he tells me he's visited you while you've been here," the doctor added.

"Oh, yes. Of course, never when Mom might pop

in. I hate being juggled between the two of them like a bouncing tennis ball. It wears a person out."

"Is that how you feel? Like a tennis ball?"

"Sometimes. It's better that they're divorced, you know. Our house was like living in a pressure chamber all the time."

"And now? How is it now at your home?"

"All right, I guess. More peaceful." She gazed toward the window. The afternoon sun was slanting through the partially closed blinds and casting striped shadows along the wall of Dr. Rosenberg's office. Although the shadows were horizontal, they still reminded Lacey of prison bars. Suddenly, without warning, her eyes filled with tears. "I miss being a family," she said softly.

"Your dad says he sees you often. Is that true?"

"He calls it 'dates.' He's taken me to a play and a few movies, then out to dinner. But it's not easy to make time, because I have things to do at school and he travels."

"Don't you enjoy the time together with him?"

"I don't want a date with my dad." Lacey sniffed and wiped away the moisture gathered in the corners of her eyes. "I want us all to live together. Be together."

"But you also said the two of them can't get along when they live together."

"So why can't they? Other people do. What's so hard about working out problems so that you can live with someone?"

"Are you angry at your parents because they can't get along?"

Many times, she'd been disgusted with them, irritated at their inability to communicate and work out their differences. She remembered the trip up to Jenny House the previous summer. They'd fought and argued the whole way, and by the time she'd arrived, she felt ready to throw something. It was no wonder that when she'd marched into the room determined not to stay around a bunch of sick kids all summer, and Katie had come on like Miss Congeniality that Lacey had snapped at her and sulked the first few days. "I guess I am angry at them," Lacey told Dr. Rosenberg. "I know kids my age who can get along with one another better than my parents can at their age."

"And how about the divorce? Are you angry about that too?"

This was a more difficult question to answer because her feelings went deeper than anger. It was an anger coupled with a sense of helplessness. "I've already said that the divorce made life more hassle-free for us."

"But does it make you *angry?*"

"Yes," she admitted. "I don't want to be part of a broken home. Whenever kids at school talk about their families, it bothers me because they have two parents living together and I don't."

"Surely some of them come from single-parent families. Or maybe step families."

She thought of the people she really cared about —Jeff, Terri, Katie, Chelsea—they all lived with both their parents. Even Todd had parents who'd remained married. She looked at Dr. Rosenberg. "I know there are lots of kids who come from split homes. But I don't like being one of them."

"So you're angry about what you can't change."

"Wouldn't you be?" she countered sharply.

He didn't answer her, but instead asked, "What have you done to let your parents know you're angry at them?"

"Nothing," she grumbled. "There's nothing I can do. They didn't ask my permission to get their divorce. So they wouldn't listen to anything I said. Or wanted."

"Often, when someone makes you angry, you want to take revenge on the someone who hurt you. That's a typical human response."

"Revenge?" Lacey scoffed. "How can somebody get even with parents who dump each other?"

"Are you certain you have no power, nothing in your control to get back at them?"

Baffled, she struggled to grasp his meaning. "I can't get even with them. There's no way."

He tapped his fingertips thoughtfully against the top of his desk, where papers had been stacked into several wire baskets. "I want you to think about what you control that they don't. Think about what you can do to make them miserable and helpless, feeling the way you felt over their divorce."

"What I control?" She puckered her brow. "I'm sixteen, I don't control—" She stopped talking as insight washed over her in a flash. She glared at him, feeling he'd tricked her, made her think of something that was outrageous and farfetched. "My diabetes," she said flatly. "You're saying that since I control my diabetes, I used it against my parents. That's not true!" She stood up, knocking over her chair.

He looked up at her and took her hand. "It's your most potent weapon, Lacey. Don't be too offended by the suggestion. Would it surprise you to know, diabetic patients use it quite often?"

"That doesn't make any sense." She was fairly shouting at the doctor. "Losing control of my diabetes on purpose hurt only *me!* I'm the one who ended up in the hospital."

His round, Santalike features lit up with a smile. "Ahhh! How right you are."

She was still mad over his suggestion. "I'm telling you that was never once in my mind when I—" She stopped her denial cold.

"When you what?" Dr. Rosenberg asked. "Come on, Lacey, tell me what you did."

She righted the chair and sat down heavily, all the fight gone out of her. "I was going to tell you anyway. I know I blew my control, but only because I wanted to lose weight, not get even with my parents."

"How did you choose to diet?"

"I juggled my insulin doses." Her heart pounded as she confessed where she'd made mistakes. She took a deep breath and added, "And sometimes, if I ate the wrong stuff, I'd make myself throw up."

He nodded, but no expression of shock or disgust crossed his face. "Would you believe that close to thirty-five percent of diabetic women have eating disorders?"

"I don't have an eating disorder."

Dr. Rosenberg continued speaking, his voice calm and nonjudgmental. "Anorexia nervosa and bulimia nervosa are two disorders that plague women eighteen to forty-five. Most often it's teens who have the problem. Binge eating and the guilt it causes is bad enough in the general population, but in the diabetic it's disastrous. It wreaks havoc with blood sugar levels and metabolism. It's often life threatening. You were lucky this time."

She fiddled with a piece of paper on the edge of his desk rather than look at him directly. "I hate being fat."

"According to weight charts, your weight's well within normal limits and has been for years. Maybe it's the fashion industry that gives you girls an unrealistic message about body weight and appearance, but so many women cling to the idea that thin is better."

"Sometimes I feel fat," Lacey argued.

"And when Type I diabetes is diagnosed, it's usually after the patient is in the grip of keto and has become greatly dehydrated. Once insulin levels are restored, the patient experiences rapid weight gain and rehydration. Unfortunately, a lot of women get scared because they're fearful of becoming overweight. So they begin a regime of insulin manipulation and purging to knock off what they think is excess weight."

"It's easier to lose weight if you give yourself less insulin," Lacey said defensively. "Especially if you eat the wrong stuff."

"But didn't Sue explain to you that there are no wrong foods for you to eat? You just have to plan for them."

"And what fun it is," Lacey declared, her tone edged with sarcasm. "All your friends are partying and eating anything they want, and you're stuck with your meal plan."

"People with illnesses have to make compromises. Much like people who are married and can't get along," he said quietly.

His logic had brought her full circle. Her parents had never learned the art of compromise and now, if she was going to manage her diabetes, she would have to become a master of compromise. Lacey suddenly felt tired and defeated. There was no way to win this war, she decided. Jeff's words about asking and knowing why something happened returned to her. He was correct—the answers couldn't *change* anything. They could only help a person to perhaps understand and learn to live with whatever happens.

She looked straight at the doctor. "I don't plan to mess up again. I won't force myself to throw up anymore."

"I don't think you're a true bulimic, Lacey," Dr. Rosenberg said, tilting back in his chair. "I think you got caught up in something and it got out of control. But you're smarter now and you have a whole team of professionals who want the best for you. You're intelligent, bright, and very attractive. There's no reason in the world that you can't control your diabetes instead of it controlling you."

He stood, took both her hands, and pulled her to her feet. "And speaking of controlling, your parents are out of your hands too. They've made their choices for their lives. But you have many choices ahead of you. Make the ones that will bring you health and happiness."

If only it were that simple, she thought. But at the moment happiness seemed like a recipe for which she didn't have the ingredients. Nor was she certain where to begin looking for them. "I'll try," she told Dr. Rosenberg. "I promise . . . I'll try."

Seventeen

Her uncle gave her permission to leave the hospital long enough to go out with Jeff on a date. Jeff took her to a quiet, romantic restaurant, where she carefully chose a dinner of all the right foods, prepared in all the right ways, from the menu.

Afterward, they walked hand in hand in Biscayne Park on a promenade that ran parallel to Biscayne Bay. The night was balmy and a light tropical breeze stirred the palm fronds overhead. A full moon shone across the water, and in the distance they could see the huge Caribbean cruise ships at anchor.

Lacey told Jeff about most of her session with Dr. Rosenberg, excluding the part concerning purging. She decided the image of her forcing herself to vomit wasn't very romantic, and besides, she was ashamed of what she'd done.

She asked, "Do you think he could be right about me being mad at my parents and using my diabetes to get back at them? I'd hate to think my subconscious mind could make me do something like that."

"Shrinks love all that subconscious stuff," Jeff said. His smile looked sexy in the moonlight. "But it's true that sometimes we act in ways we don't mean to. I think we make excuses for ourselves because it's easier than changing the way we're acting."

"Well, I didn't set out to get even with them, but when I was sick at least they stopped fighting with each other. For once they were concentrating on me and not themselves."

Jeff nodded in understanding. He asked, "Has your uncle said anything about when you might go home?"

"Another day or so. 'Course, I still have to meet with Dr. Rosenberg even after I leave the hospital. And there's no way I can get out of attending one of the support groups Uncle Nelson's been wanting me to join."

"That shouldn't be so bad."

Lacey wrinkled her nose. "I'm just not crazy about the idea, that's all. He says that when the institute opens, it'll have plenty of programs and stuff to do. I promised him I'd be a regular little girl scout." She saluted smartly.

"You're always such a good sport," Jeff joked. "I don't see why your uncle puts up with you."

They strolled over to a bench that fronted the bay, and Jeff pulled Lacey down next to him and draped his arms over the back of the wooden slats. The moonlight glittered on the water and reminded her of sparkling jewels. "Amanda used to say that moonlight and starlight were really fairy dust," Lacey observed softly.

"Do you think about her much?"

"I think about Jenny House and about what a good time I had while I was there. Did you know I went back for a visit during Thanksgiving weekend?" Lacey asked.

"No, I didn't. Why?"

"Katie sent me an airline ticket. Chelsea wanted all of us together when she and her new friend Jillian went to Jenny House.

"And Katie paid your way?"

"Yes . . . with some of her Wish money." The mention of Katie sent a shadow across Lacey's heart.

"That Katie's something else," Jeff said. "I've never known anybody quite like her."

Lacey felt a lump swell in her throat. "I miss her, Jeff."

"Haven't you patched things up with her yet?"

Lacey shook her head. "I don't know how."

"You pick up the phone and tell her you're sorry. You are sorry, aren't you?" When she nodded, he said, "What's so hard?" He glanced down the sidewalk toward Bay Walk, the trendy shopping area located in the park, adjacent to the bay. "Come on." He took her hand and pulled her behind him.

"Where are we going?"

"To the nearest pay phone. You call Katie right now."

Lacey felt her mouth go dry as soon as she dialed Katie's number using Jeff's calling card. "She's probably not home," Lacey told Jeff as she listened to Katie's phone ringing in Michigan. "She's probably off doing something with Josh—Katie! Hi, how are you?"

"Lacey?"

Katie's voice sounded so familiar and sweet that Lacey almost started crying. "Yes, it's me."

An awkward silence stretched between them. Katie broke it by asking, "So are you out of the hospital yet?"

"Almost. I—I've been working out some stuff with my doctors. I—uh—have diabetes, you know."

"*I* know. Are you sure you do?"

"I do now." Jeff nudged her in the side, and Lacey shot him a look that said *Don't rush me.* Lacey squeezed the phone receiver tightly because her hand was perspiring. "I'm sorry, Katie," she blurted out. "I'm sorry about our fight on the phone when you called me at the hospital. You were right about everything you said."

"I didn't mean to sound unsympathetic," Katie apologized. "I got angry and I shouldn't have . . . especially with you so sick. But, Lacey, I've never seen anybody deny the obvious the way you do."

"Well, I'm not denying it anymore." She cut her

eyes sideways. Jeff gave her a grin and a thumbs-up signal. "Guess who's here with me?" Lacey said into the receiver. "Jeff."

"No lie? How did that happen? Have you changed your mind about him?"

"I can't discuss it now; he's standing right here." She hoped Katie wouldn't pump her for more information. Katie was the only person in the world who knew how Lacey *really* felt about Jeff, and she didn't want it to all come out. Especially when Jeff was treating her more like a friend and sister than a girlfriend. He still hadn't made a move to kiss her or be romantic with her the way he had at Jenny House or the beach party.

"Hey, Katie!" Jeff yelled into the mouthpiece of the receiver.

"Tell him hi from me," Katie said with a laugh. "And when you can, call me and give me every single detail of what's going on. I can tell we have a lot of catching up to do."

"So you're not mad at me anymore?"

"I could never stay mad at you, Lacey. We're 'forever friends,' remember?"

Forever friends was the way Jenny Crawford had signed her Wish letter. "I remember," Lacey said, feeling as if a ton weight had been lifted off her heart. "How's track going?"

"We're smoking everybody." Katie's voice sounded all smiles. "My team's coming to that track meet in Miami in May for sure." It seemed ages before that Katie had mentioned the national event to Lacey. "You'll come cheer for us, won't you?"

"You bet. I'll bring Jeff with me. Will Josh come with you?"

"Our men's team isn't going to qualify, but Josh will come anyway as our coach's helper. There'll be several college coaches at the meet scouting us contenders. If I'm ever going to be offered a scholarship, this will be the time."

"That's great. I hope you do get an offer. So, are you and Josh doing okay now?"

Katie's abrupt silence spoke volumes to Lacey. "We'll talk more later," Katie said.

Lacey told Katie that Chelsea had written and that she sounded fine, they promised to call each other again over the weekend, and Lacey hung up. She turned to Jeff, smiled, and said, "Katie still loves me. Thanks for making me call her and get things straightened out."

He bowed from the waist. "McKensie's friendship-mending agency at your service."

Impulsively, she threw her arms around his neck. She held tight, hoping he'd hold her and kiss her under the beautiful moon. He only gave her a quick squeeze and then unwrapped her arms. "Come on, I'd better get you back to the hospital before your uncle sends out a search party."

"Sure," she said, forcing lightness into her step as she walked beside him toward the car. But inside, Lacey felt as if she'd been slugged in the stomach and left without any breath. Jeff had all but brushed her off. He didn't want her. And it seemed unlikely that he'd ever want her again.

*   *   *

The day Lacey was supposed to go home from the hospital her father was out of town on business and her mother had an important presentation for a client at the ad agency. "I'll simply tell them I can't attend," her mother told Lacey.

"No way. Jeff will drive me home. It's not like I'm sick, you know. I'll just go home, get my room in order, and get ready to go back to school tomorrow. I'll start supper too."

They agreed on the arrangement, and when her uncle came in with the final paperwork, Jeff took her belongings down to his car. "I'm glad to be getting out of here," she said.

"And I'm glad you're doing well enough to go home." He eyed her. "You still need to put on about ten pounds."

"I know. I'm starting a workout program at a nearby gym. I'll probably look muscle-bound by the summer. The therapist suggested I take up tennis too."

"Stop griping. It'll be good for you. I want you in my office at the end of next week. I want to keep tabs on you."

She knew she was going to have to prove herself before everyone would trust her totally with her management again. "I have a favor to ask," she said.

"Name it."

"A while back, Dr. Rosenberg volunteered to send me on a tour of the new Diabetes Research Institute. I told him no, but I've changed my mind."

"You want to scope out the building? It's not finished, you know. But the PR director is downstairs, and I'm sure he'd be pleased to take you and Jeff through the place. He's very savvy about the newest developments in diabetes research."

"Good. I've been looking at the building for days out of Dr. Rosenberg's window, and I'm curious. I want to know what all you medical brains are doing to get rid of diabetes once and for all. I want to know if I'll ever be cured of this lousy disease."

Eighteen

"Excuse the dust. These are the finishing touches. We hope to open next month," Gary Kleiman, the publicity and education director of the DRI, explained to Lacey and Jeff as he stepped around a pile of ceiling insulation and led the way inside the Diabetes Research Institute.

The scent of new building materials and fresh paint filled the spacious lobby of the enormous structure. Lacey watched two workers as they busily placed slabs of tile along a corridor. She ducked around a ladder where a carpenter was standing pounding nails into a window frame.

"Pretty impressive," Jeff said, looking up from the center of the giant atrium. Soaring white pillars and concrete walkways stretched overhead.

"Reminds me of a luxury hotel," Lacey said. "You sure this is for medical research?"

Gary laughed. "Come upstairs with me. I'll show you the research floors." All the way up on the elevator, he talked of the visionary goals of the DRI. This was the site for research, education, and treatment, and they hoped to attract the foremost scientists in the world. "We'll have a day care room for the staff's and workers' children. There'll be all kinds of programs and seminars. Patients will get the newest and best treatments. Our medical library will be one the finest. It will tie in with other medical libraries via computers."

For the first time, Lacey became aware of the tremendous effort that was going into finding a cure for diabetes. Gary took them through labs where state of the art laboratory equipment and computers sat waiting to begin their duties. Lacey heard about sophisticated machines that cost hundreds of thousands of dollars; money raised by donations, charity balls, and sporting events; research grants; and highway "hold-ups," where parents of diabetics stood at busy intersections and collected from motorists. She saw firsthand the rooms where technicians would conduct meticulous experiments.

"We know how to cure diabetes, you know," Gary said.

"Then why haven't I been cured? I hate getting shots every day."

Gary smiled and nodded. "We all do."

"You're a diabetic too?"

"Ever since I was six. Over the years I've been

treated for advanced retinopathy, and now I'm classified as legally blind. I had a kidney transplant seven years ago after years of dialysis."

The information sent a chill through Lacey. Was this to be her future too? "Tell me about a cure," she said.

"Actually, there are several programs throughout the country dedicated to finding a cure. But the one the DRI is most avidly pursuing is islet cell transplantation."

Lacey explained to Jeff that islet cells were responsible for insulin production within the pancreas.

Gary added, "In the diabetic, the islets stop doing their job. And without insulin the body can't convert food into glucose. In essence, the diabetic can be eating like a horse and still starving to death."

"So why can't you put these islet cells back inside me?" Lacey asked.

"That's what we're trying to do. Scientists affiliated with the DRI have been working on this for over twenty years, but it's a complex task. In the seventies we transplanted insulin-producing islet cells into diabetic rats. In the eighties we did the same thing with dogs. Both experiments worked. In 1985 we tried it on humans. One patient had a very acceptable response."

"You mean you cured her diabetes? Then why aren't you doing this for me?"

Gary shook his head. "Believe me, if it were that easy, *I'd* have been transplanted by now. Eventually, the graft of new islets failed in the patient. But doctors think it was because we didn't transplant enough into her. We gave her approximately eighty thousand cells. Now we realize a person needs closer to eight hundred thousand to a million islet cells in order to function normally."

"That's a lot of cells," Jeff said.

"And that vast a number is part of our problem."

"How do you mean?"

"Where do we get them?"

Lacey pondered the question. She remembered Katie and Chelsea and their donor organs. "From donors?" she asked Gary.

"True, but preserving a donor pancreas outside the body is difficult. So first our scientists had to solve that problem. Then they had to isolate the islet cells. Remember, the pancreas does more in the body than just produce insulin.

"They discovered a new enzyme to improve the isolation process. They designed a machine to help isolate and purify the yield of cells from a single pancreas. Then, of course, they have to deal with transplantation's major nemesis—rejection."

Lacey recalled the medications Katie took to impede rejection of her transplanted heart. "But has anybody really been cured for always?"

"There is an islet transplant recipient in Kentucky who'd had her pancreas removed for other medical reasons, and she's been implanted. Actually the liver is a good host for new islet cells—and guess what? They've been working fine for three years."

"Then why can't you and I get these new islet

cells?" Lacey's curiosity had turned into genuine, hope-filled interest.

"That's our next step and the primary focus of new research." Gary punched the elevator button to take them down to the ground floor. "We know that diabetes is caused by a combination of factors. A genetic predisposition, a virus, and a person's own immune system." Gary ticked the causes off on his fingers.

"So even if we transplant healthy islets into a patient, we don't know if diabetes will occur again. And if we transplant a patient, he must take immunosuppressant drugs to avoid rejection. As a person who's been taking these drugs for my kidney transplant, I can tell you, they aren't without their long-term side effects. Brittle bones and excessive hair growth to name a couple." He rubbed the top of his head which was partially bald. "Except on the head. Why can't I grow hair up here?"

Lacey and Jeff laughed, which broke some of the intensity of the discussion. "I don't care if I grow hair out of my feet," Lacey declared. "It would be worth it to get rid of all the shots."

"I've read stuff about cloning," Jeff said as the elevator opened on the ground floor. "Why can't you grow islet cells like in a lab or something? You know, on an islet farm."

Lacey gave him a patronizing look and asked, "Like in Old MacDonald's islet farm, eee-aye-eee-aye-oh?"

"That is precisely what we're trying to do," Gary said. "Actually, trying to come up with close to a million cells for every diabetic in the world is impossible to do with donor organs. And if we can grow them, we can avoid the rejection problem because they won't be genetically preprogrammed."

Lacey interrupted. "Let me guess. It's hard to grow them."

"Bingo!" Gary said. "Someday we may be able to grow them in abundance in petri dishes, but we're not even close to that technology today. So now we're experimenting with using pigs as surrogate hosts."

"Pigs?" Lacey and Jeff asked in unison.

"Believe it or not, the little oinkers are frighteningly close to humans in their genetic makeup."

Lacey shot Jeff a sideways glance. "I'm not surprised."

"Is that a rude comment about my gender?" he asked.

"Did I say anything?" She blinked innocently, then turned back to Gary. "So how will pigs help the cause?"

"We hope they can be used as hosts to grow the cells, which can be extracted and transplanted into diabetics. At least that's the theory. More testing has to be done to see if it's a practical solution."

Lacey's head swam with information. Every time something gave her hope, another piece of information came along to dash it. "So you're still a long way off from curing *my* diabetes," she said.

"A lot closer than we were," Gary told her. "The institute's main purpose is to put itself out of business. How many other organizations can claim as much?"

"And how about artificial pancreases?" Jeff asked. "Can't they make a machine for you to use?"

"Machines aren't living tissue," Gary said. "Who wants to be hooked to a machine? Or even have one implanted inside your body? Even if we could make it small enough, which we can't, remember the pancreas is a multifunctional organ. And islet cells are very interesting little pieces of protoplasm. For instance, they come in all different shapes and sizes. Is this important? And they not only produce insulin, they also regulate the flow of insulin into the body." He shook his head. "There's simply a lot we don't know yet."

The three of them stood in the nearly completed lobby, their mood subdued. Finally Lacey said, "I don't know if I should be excited or not. A cure seems impossible because there's so much more to be learned."

Gary squeezed her arm. "We'll lick it eventually. I'm hopeful because the human body is 'fearfully and wonderfully made.' For every dilemma we come up against, there's a solution. Time and money for research is what we need. You're young, Lacey. You'll reap the benefits of our research one of these days. In the meantime, take good care of yourself and stay in as tight a control of your blood sugar as possible to hold off the side effects."

She thought of all the damage she'd allowed to happen to her body already by mismanaging her disease. In spite of his tour and explanations, she felt depressed. "Maybe your hope will be contagious."

He smiled, and she recognized understanding in his eyes. "Two years ago I married. And last year I had a son. Every day I look at him, I find hope for the next day. As long as I'm alive, I'll hang on to that hope."

She felt Jeff ease his arm around her waist and knew he was feeling sympathy for her. She eased out of his embrace because she didn't want his sympathy. She wanted his love.

Lacey thanked Gary for his time, then asked Jeff to please drive her home. They left the concrete and glass monument to diabetes research and headed for the parking garage under the blazing Miami sun. Lacey knew someone like Todd would never have been caring enough to listen to Gary, and even ask questions. A person didn't have to be sick to understand, but it still made Lacey uneasy to call herself sick.

Nineteen

Lacey held her head high as she walked down the hall at school, her gaze focused straight ahead. She avoided eye contact with everyone because she was certain that everybody in the school was discussing her. And her diabetes.

"It's a big school," Jeff had reminded her the night before as he'd said good night. "I don't think you should be worried about being the main topic of conversation."

She'd slept fitfully, nervous about returning and facing the kids in her circle who had never known about her disease.

"Wait up!" Terri called. Lacey stopped and waited until Terri came alongside her. "I need you to come with me to the auditorium after school," Terri said, slightly out of breath.

"Why? I was going straight home after school."

"You can't spare me fifteen minutes?"

"I don't want to hang around."

"Just come with me." Before Lacey could beg off, the bell rang and Terri dashed away. She called over her shoulder, "See you at three."

At three Lacey went to the auditorium only because Terri had been a good friend to her during her ordeal. She pushed the heavy door open and saw that the vast room was empty. Onstage, the curtain had been pulled open and there was a single chair lit with a spotlight. Curious, Lacey hugged her books closer and walked down the sloping floor to the stage. She climbed the steps, crossed to the chair, and saw a sign taped to the seat. She read: SIT HERE.

Lacey glanced around for Terri. All at once, from backstage, a throng of kids surged forward, Terri leading the pack. In unison they yelled, "Surprise!"

Lacey stood immobile as the cast and crew of the play swarmed around her. "Did we surprise you?" Maria asked.

"Did you suspect anything?" Terri wanted to know.

Lacey shot Terri a glance that could kill. "I'm surprised, all right," she said.

"Good." Terri ignored her expression and grabbed her arm. "Come backstage. We have a party all set up."

Farther back and to one side there was a table heaped with vegetable trays, diet sodas, and a magnificent fruit platter decorated with a sign reading:

WELCOME BACK, LACEY. Ms. Kasch hugged Lacey warmly. "It's wonderful to have you back in school. We've been concerned, but Terri has kept us well informed. I called the hospital switchboard all through spring break to check on you personally. You gave us quite a fright on opening night."

Others came forward and hugged Lacey too. Two of the group told her about a friend and a parent who had diabetes. "If you'd ever had a reaction, I'd have known exactly what to do," a girl named Gloria assured her.

Lacey felt overwhelmed by the attention and concern. She had expected shunning, not understanding. "I'm sorry I loused up opening night," Lacey told them.

"The show went on," Ms. Kasch said. "But we sure missed you."

"We missed your makeup," Gordon called out. "I did my own and I looked more like Freddy Krueger than the character I was playing."

Laughter rippled through the group.

"Let's eat," someone suggested, and kids scattered toward the food table.

At first Lacey felt uncomfortable with everyone restricted to eating the foods best for her. But no one appeared to care as they piled paper plates high with raw vegetables, dips, crackers, and fruit. She also realized that even if the table had been overflowing with sweets and goodies, she could have taken a taste of whatever she wanted without feeling guilty. Tastes were okay. Pigging out wasn't.

Lacey turned when the side stage door swung

open and sunlight spilled inside. "Are we late?" Todd asked as he sauntered in, his arm around Monet's waist.

"Yes, you're late," Ms. Kasch said. Her look of disapproval caused Todd to release his hold on Monet.

Lacey felt herself tense, but she pointedly ignored Todd and walked over to Terri, who was busily rummaging for paper napkins in a grocery sack.

"Sorry about him," Terri said as she pulled out the package of napkins. "But Ms. Kasch insisted all the kids come to your party. I didn't actually invite him, but of course, word got around."

"No problem," Lacey said. "I'm completely over him." She watched Todd make the rounds of the different groups, noticing how he constantly vied for the attention of the others and how his manners bordered on rudeness. She thought about Jeff and recalled the way he'd held her, letting her cry, talking to her, and making her feel special. She wondered how she could have ever been so stupid as to want to date a guy like Todd.

He came toward her. She lifted her head and gave him her frostiest stare. "I'm glad to see you," he said. "I was going to visit you in the hospital, but I went skiing with my folks in Aspen. I was out of town while you were sick."

"I had plenty to keep me busy," she said.

"So you aren't mad?"

"I'm not mad," she said, meaning it. "Being mad implies I care. And I don't care." She watched the expression on his face shift as her words sank in.

But before he could say anything, she added, "Have a good life, Todd," and turned away.

"Good putdown," Terri told her.

"I meant every word," Lacey said. She went with Terri to the food table and chose an assortment of vegetables and fruit.

She looked up to see Monet standing on the opposite side of the table. Their gazes clashed. Dark half circles rimmed Monet's eyes, and her skin didn't radiate a healthy glow. To any other observer, Monet was still quite pretty, but Lacey knew Monet's secret. Suddenly, Lacey felt sorry for the girl.

Monet said, "I was sorry to hear you're sick."

"I'm not sick," Lacey told her. "I have diabetes. And at least I'm on top of *my* problem."

Monet's gaze darted anxiously from side to side, looking to see if anyone might be overhearing the conversation. "Are you saying *I* have a problem?"

Lacey nodded. "You know you do, and it'll catch up with you sooner or later."

"Butt out," Monet said tersely. She turned on her heel and stalked away.

"What was that all about?" Terri asked. Curiosity all but leaked from her pores.

"I can't say."

"Why not? What's going on? Come on . . . tell me."

Lacey shook her head. "Let's just say that Monet is headed for big-time trouble." Lacey was certain that Monet was bulimic and had been for some time. And she knew from her sessions with Dr. Rosenberg that Monet needed therapy to deal with her eating disorder. Still, Lacey doubted that Monet would listen to a word Lacey had to say on the subject. All her feelings of dislike for Monet dissolved as she realized how desperate Monet must be to force herself to vomit to remain thin rather than accept herself as she was.

Lacey turned toward Terri and asked, "So, isn't there anything chocolate at this party?"

"You can still eat chocolate?" Terri asked.

"Sure, as long as I'm smart about it."

Terri grinned. "Terrific. I'd hate to think you had to go through the rest of your life without chocolate."

"Me too." She glanced toward Monet, who was clinging to Todd's hand. "But there are worse things to go through life without," Lacey said. To herself, she added, *Like self-respect.*

"You look wonderful, honey."

"You're my dad. Of course you think I look good."

Lacey was sitting across from her father in a restaurant, the aromas of charbroiled steaks filling the air.

"How's school going?"

"Fine. The stay in the hospital didn't put me far behind at all. I'm even ahead in some courses. Did I mention that my friend Katie's coming for a track meet next month? I'm really looking forward to seeing her." She sensed he wanted to have a heart-to-heart talk and she wasn't sure she felt like having one, especially in a restaurant.

"I'm sorry if I did anything to cause your problem with your diabetes," he finally said.

"You've been talking to Dr. Rosenberg, haven't you?"

"We've had several discussions."

"And you're feeling guilty about my diabetes." He looked startled, and Lacey said, "I've had this same conversation with Mom. Look, I don't hold you or Mom responsible for passing along bad genes to me. And I don't feel responsible for your divorce either."

Even in the dim light she could tell his face had reddened. "I know Dr. Rosenberg feels the marital problems between Mom and me contributed to your failure to manage your diabetes properly. I never thought our problems would affect you so much. It never occurred to me that our fights would cause you grief."

"They did," she admitted. "But I didn't deliberately sabotage my control to get even with the two of you. Although it was nice having both of you with me at the hospital. Like a real family."

"Lacey, I can't go back and undo the damage. I only hope that someday you'll understand." He lifted her chin with his forefinger. "You do know that no matter what, I love you. And I always will."

She nodded. "I know how you both feel about me. What bothered me was why you couldn't ever love each other." A film of moisture formed in her eyes.

"I have no excuses for you. Only that some people shouldn't be together. I'm sorry if we hurt you."

Sorry. That word appeared to be the most often used to Lacey's way of thinking. She was a diabetic. Her parents were divorced. Her best friends lived daily with the threat of imminent death. Everyone was sorry, but nothing was going to change the facts. "I'm sorry too, Dad. So, I guess there's nothing to do but keep on keeping on." She dabbed her eyes with the corner of her linen napkin.

"What will you do this summer?" her father asked, changing the subject. "There'll be some openings in my office for temporary help. Would you like to interview for a position?"

She shook her head. Until that moment she hadn't been sure what she wanted to do. Now she did know. "I got a letter from Mr. Holloway last week inviting me to be a counselor," she told her father. "That's what I want to do. I want to go back to Jenny House for the summer."

Twenty

⸌⸍

THE NATIONAL HIGH school track competition was to be held in the Orange Bowl, and competitors from all over the country began arriving in Miami for the three-day meet early in the final week of May. After Katie called Lacey to say she and her teammates were settled into their hotel rooms, Lacey called Jeff and together they drove to the hotel.

Josh termed the girls' reunion "earth-shaking" and "eardrum splitting" when the four of them met in the lobby, and after the squealing and hugging stopped, Josh took Jeff to see the beach so that Lacey and Katie could visit with each other in private.

"You look *fab*," Katie said once they'd tucked themselves away in a corner of the busy lobby.

"Not as good as you," Lacey insisted. Katie fairly

glowed with good health. Her lean, long-limbed body looked fit and tight. Her long, dark hair was held at the nape of her neck by a tortoiseshell barrette, and her pretty blue eyes sparkled.

"Tell me the truth, is your diabetes really back in good control?"

"I'm struggling," Lacey admitted. "You're the only one I'm telling this to, but I did some damage to myself these past few months. My doctors are insisting on extra monitoring of my kidneys and eyes because some of the tests show problem areas. I'll have another complete workup in the fall to see how I'm progressing."

A worried frown creased Katie's face. "I'm sorry."

Lacey dismissed her concern with a wave of her hand. "No more about me. Let's talk about you. Are you all set for the big meet?"

"Ready and willing. This is my big chance, Lacey. The coach from Arizona sent word that he's come especially to see me run. It's important that I do well."

"You'll leave them all in your dust."

"I want a scholarship offer more than anything."

"So you'd go away for sure?"

A frown crossed Katie's face. "It'll be a hard choice, but I think I can persuade my folks."

"And Josh?"

"That'll be harder."

Lacey saw tension in Katie's expression. "You still love him, don't you?"

"I'll always love him. That's what makes it so difficult."

"And Garrison?"

Katie sighed and picked at the upholstery of her chair. "He still makes my knees quiver. But I keep him at arm's length because Josh is so jealous."

"A real dilemma," Lacey observed. "I'm personally acquainted with the knee-quivering effect." An overhead fan rustled the fronds of the giant potted palm beside her chair.

"Josh wants me to marry him."

"What!" Lacey bolted upright.

"Not right away. He's going to the University of Michigan this fall and he feels that if we both go there, we can also work and save enough money to get married by our senior year."

"But that's not what you want, is it?"

Katie eyes clouded. "There's so much I want. I want to run track. I want to live on my own. I want to date Garrison. I want to marry Josh. I want it *all*."

"And I thought I had tough decisions to make."

"Such as?"

"Such as the best way to make Jeff fall in love with me again."

"I'm sure he's still crazy about you."

"He doesn't act like it." Lacey dipped her head, spilling her long blond hair forward. "He hasn't so much as kissed me since I was in the hospital. Last January—when I had my big chance with him—I flubbed it. Now he's nice to me, but he doesn't feel the same way he did last summer at Jenny House. I can tell."

Katie drummed her fingers on the arm of the chair. "You burned him, Lacey. And he may think that you'll run hot and cold on him again. Especially if he has a bleeding episode. Besides, you did brush him off for Todd."

"I'm not that way now." Lacey's plea sounded impassioned. "I really, really like him. I'm all through with Todd and his kind. I want Jeff."

"At least you live in the same city. What's he doing this summer?"

Lacey gave Katie a cagey sideways glance. "He's going to take a counselor job at Jenny House. And so am I."

"Chelsea's going back too."

Lacey smiled. "I'll bet Mr. Holloway invited you to come also."

"He did."

"Will you?"

"I've really thought hard about it. It might be the best way to put distance between me and Ann Arbor, between me and Garrison and Josh. Maybe I could sort things out better if I weren't constantly bombarded with pressure."

"There's another reason too." Lacey poked Katie in the knee with her finger to emphasis her point. "We made a promise to each other that we'd meet there this summer. For Amanda. And for Jillian."

"I haven't forgotten."

In her mind's eye, Lacey could see the hand-built memorial they'd erected for their dead friends atop the mountain. "I wonder if Jillian's earring is still in place." She envisioned the sparkling diamond stud Jillian had put in the faded photograph of Katie, Chelsea, Lacey, and Amanda.

"Or if the fairies have stolen it away?" Katie suggested.

"There's only one way to find out," Lacey declared.

"You could write and tell me."

"Nope. You'll have to come and check it out for yourself."

"That's blackmail."

Lacey grinned. "I know."

Jeff and Josh walked up. Josh sat on the arm of Katie's chair, put his arm around her shoulders, and kissed the top of her head.

Lacey longed for Jeff to be affectionate toward her, but he settled on a nearby sofa table, across from the two chairs.

Josh glanced at his watch. "Curfew time. Coach said team members had to be locked in their rooms by eleven."

Lacey and Jeff promised to be in the stands for the opening ceremony on Thursday night, and the four of them said their good-byes. Lacey talked nonstop on the ride home, telling Jeff that she was certain she'd talk Katie into coming to Jenny House for the summer. "It'll be just like old times," she told Jeff when he walked her to her front door.

"What makes you think so?" Moonlight and shadow flicked over him.

"Because that's the way I want it to be. Like old times." Her heart began to hammer. She wanted him to kiss her so badly, she ached inside. She thought about kissing him first, but fought the urge. No . . . if he wanted her, he'd have to make the first move. She'd simply have to make him want her.

"But a whole year's gone past. Things change," he said quietly. "People change."

Lacey couldn't bear to hear the rejection in his message. "Sometimes people change for the better," she countered.

He shrugged, then said, "Finals begin soon, so I'll be putting in a lot of study time."

"No time for me?"

"Not as much," he admitted. "Once finals are over, I'm going home to see Mom and Dad."

Lacey's heart sank. "So I probably won't see much of you until we both get to North Carolina."

"I guess not."

"I'll write," she offered.

"You never have before," he reminded her.

"I will this time."

He took her hand and placed a kiss in her palm. She wished it had been on her mouth. "I'll pick you up for the track meet Thursday."

Feeling frustrated, she watched him drive away. The night grew quiet. Lacey stood on her front porch and gazed up at the sky. Stars gleamed above her, making her feel small, alone, and sad. She wanted Jeff to love her.

But then, so had Amanda Burdick. Lacey remembered Amanda's bright smile and sunny optimism. "What do you think, Amanda?" she asked looking up at shimmering stars. "Do you mind if I go after your boyfriend?"

Her question hung in the silent night.

As she turned to go inside, she saw a shooting star arc through the darkness. In wonder, Lacey looked up. There seemed to be a glowing trail across the face of the heavens. Was it an answer sent to her from a world beyond rainbows? Lacey felt renewed hope within her heart. She'd been given a second chance for all the days of her life. Beginning now, she'd make the most of it.

Coming soon:

A Summer for Goodbye

Katie, Chelsea, and Lacey return to Jenny House, each for their own reasons. Over the summer, they face challenges and difficulties, rediscover old loves, and form new dreams. And there, an unexpected tragedy tests the bonds of their friendship and the depths of their commitments for hope in their future.